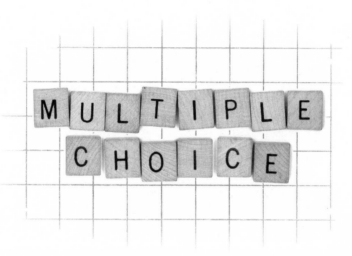

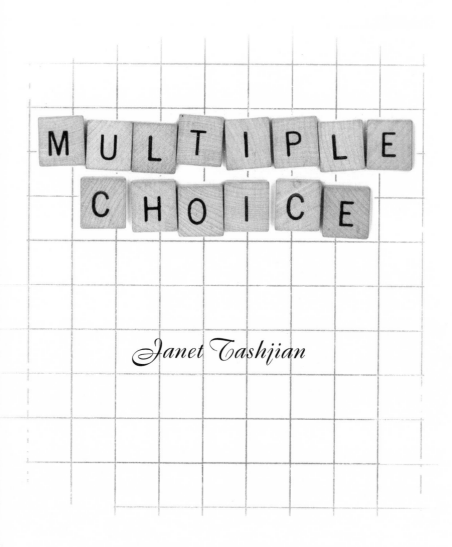

MULTIPLE CHOICE

Janet Tashjian

Henry Holt and Company ★ New York

Many thanks to:

a) All the research librarians who pointed me in the right direction—especially Kathy Killeen in Needham

b) Brendan Connell for his anagram expertise

c) Arlyne Harrower for nurturing my love of language

d) Wilfred Lajoie for instilling a love of games and puzzles

e) Luke Rhinehart for sharing the gift of chance

Henry Holt and Company, Inc.
Publishers since 1866
115 West 18th Street
New York, New York 10011

Henry Holt is a registered trademark of Henry Holt and Company, Inc.

Library of Congress Cataloging-in-Publication Data
Tashjian, Janet. Multiple choice / Janet Tashjian.
p. cm.
Summary: Monica, a fourteen-year-old perfectionist and word game expert,
tries to break free from all the suffocating rules in her life by creating a
game for living called Multiple Choice.
[1. Obsessive-compulsive disorder—Fiction. 2. Mental illness—Fiction.
3. Self-perception—Fiction. 4. Word games—Fiction.] I. Title.
PZ7.T211135Mu 1999 [Fic]—dc21 98-43349

ISBN 0-8050-6086-3 / First Edition—1999
Printed in the United States of America on acid-free paper. ∞
1 3 5 7 9 10 8 6 4 2

For Pint

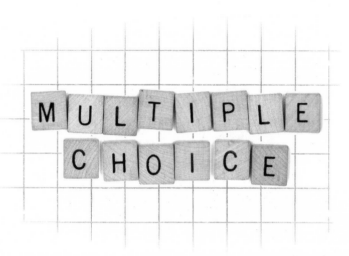

I wish my brain were a toaster.

That way I could use it when I wanted to, and when I was done, I could pull the plug and shut it off.

The reason I'm thinking about this is that I've just finished conducting a very important experiment. And after weeks of compiling and analyzing data, I have come to a scientific conclusion.

98.762 percent of my time is spent obsessing.

About what?

Everything.

Saying the wrong thing, doing the wrong thing, wearing the wrong clothes . . . I've been professionally obsessing for as long as I can remember.

I'm sure everyone obsesses; it's just a matter of degree. But is it normal to constantly think about the word you got wrong in a spelling bee back in fifth grade? (The word was *mediocre*—I still can't say it out loud.) Is it normal to stare at the broken globe in your geography class as if it magically got fixed since the last time you stared at it three minutes ago? To obsess that the girl sitting next to you in English is thinking about how your socks don't match your pants? My scientific experiment proved that I am spending 98.762 percent of my life *analyzing* my life.

I daydream about how carefree my life would be if I *could* shut my brain off like a toaster. No wearing special socks on days I have tests (black for history, blue for math); no fighting with the cafeteria ladies about slopping the food on my plate according to color (green does not go next to orange; I'm sorry). A world where I breeze from one activity to another, not worried about committing some critical error that sends the entire planet screeching to a halt. I can't help but smile at the thought.

My utopian toaster world is interrupted when Mr. Bergeron asks us to write an essay off the top of our heads about three items we would put in a time capsule for the next millennium. I come up with an answer—television, a stone from the Berlin Wall, penicillin—but most of my time is spent trying to figure out what he expects (and how he's going to grade us, of course). I approach his desk to ask him specifically what he's looking for, but he just smiles and tells me to do my best and not worry. (Excuse me, Mr. Bergeron. Perhaps I should share the results of my recent experiment with you. Ah, never mind.)

After that sad excuse for a pop quiz, my best friend, Lynn Kelly, and I walk to my locker. She blows the tips of her index fingers as if they're smoking guns. "Was that the easiest test or what?"

How can I tell her that my stomach is churning, that I can barely breathe, all because I'm petrified that Mr. Bergeron will think my answers are stupid? I try to explain as best I can without sounding like a weirdo.

Lynn waits patiently for me to finish. "I wrote about the Simpsons, candy corn, and strawberry lipstick," she says. "I defy anyone to tell me those aren't three good items for a time capsule." Then she looks at me and takes pity. "You have *got* to stop torturing yourself, Monica."

Tell me something I don't know.

I spin the lock clockwise three times before dialing the combination. I check the jacket of my book. Purple/history/third period. I feel myself yawning already.

I used to worry that Ms. Emerson would catch me not paying attention and bark out a "MONICA!" in front of the whole class. But I realized last week after Joey DeSalvo took off his shoes and clipped his toenails while she lectured about the Emancipation Proclamation that the chances of her singling me out are thin.

While most of the class catches up on sleep, I continue to obsess over Mr. Bergeron's quiz. Should I have chosen the computer instead of the television? Will he think I'm not serious enough? And how about something from World War II, the Holocaust, even? And I didn't mention anything about architecture or music. . . . I take out my notebook and try to take my mind off my mind.

My notebook is filled with word games, puzzles, and other personal musings. I turn to the page labeled GOOD QUALITIES/FLAWS. Three of my good qualities are listed: reliable, intelligent, and dependable (which may be the same as reliable, now that I think about it). But the list of flaws overflows from one page to the next. The four remaining flaws on the last page bother me; I erase them and copy the whole page over so all the flaws fit on one sheet. I count the lines—twenty-six of them. Worry too much, perfectionist, not creative, obsessive . . . the list goes on. It makes me wonder if my mother doesn't have a point—that I'm too hard on myself. Although I suppose that's just another flaw to add to the list.

I doodle the phrase WHAT IS MY PROBLEM? across the top of the page. I move the letters around—juggle them like balls, scramble them up until their meaning has changed. Eventually I come up with SWAMPY BIRTH MOLE, WISPY MARBLE MOTH, and PHIL MYER'S WOMBAT.

I've been playing these word games for years, but in Mr. Bergeron's class this week I learned these jumbled-up words are called anagrams. I must admit, it's something I'm quite good at. At first, I used to just move letters around, like REILRESBEUB or SLUBBREREEI for BLUEBERRIES. Then I began finding words inside BLUEBERRIES, like BEE and RISE and LIE. Gradually I found words that were true anagrams for BLUEBERRIES— RUBBER ELSIE and REBEL BRUISE. Soon the words hidden inside other words began to jump out at me—the letters moved around in my mind, waiting to be transformed. OCEAN became CANOE, LADIES became

IDEALS, HALITOSIS became LOIS HAS IT. But my grandpa is *truly* amazing; he can do even the long phrases in his head. I haven't gotten that good yet, but I am pretty fast. It's just habit from doing them with him for so long. It's a semi-meaningless skill, similar to how Lynn can rewind or fast-forward a cassette tape and stop it at the exact song she's looking for. Cool, but not too practical.

It's like I'm afraid I'm missing something if I leave the words alone. If I just write CANOE by itself and don't try to wring it out and go deeper, I might be missing some *meaning*, some hidden message, some . . . I don't know . . . revelation meant just for me. I scramble up the letters of the word OBSESSIVE to see if I can find a way to escape from it. All I come up with is EVE IS BOSS. Not much of a cure there.

Now Ms. Emerson is babbling about the weather conditions during the War of 1812. I write down I AM TRAPPED in my notebook and spend the next twenty-five minutes rearranging the letters. I come up with TAMPA PRIDE, MAD ART PIPE, and ADMIT PAPER until I finally settle on DAMP PIRATE. I draw a picture of a girl with an eye-patch and a wooden leg, wearing a striped shirt. She is standing on the deck of a ship, drying off from a wave that has soaked her through. Instead of a telescope, she's using a kaleidoscope to scan the horizon. But of course, she can't see the place she's looking for because she's too busy gazing at the small world in her hand—empty colors changing, changing, changing, going nowhere. I shiver in my seat at how much that sounds like my mind.

So right then and there I make a vow. I, Monica Devon, fourteen-year-old worrywart, do hereby solemnly swear to stop obsessing, to stop trying to be perfect, to stop trying to be . . . me.

When my mother and I leave for the mall, I fill up with anticipation. Not only because I'm spending time alone with her and we're shopping, but because no one will be happier than Mom if I stop obsessing. I decide not to tell her about my vow; my actions will speak for themselves. I roll down my window and let the wind from the highway in.

The only time I get to spend alone with my mother is when we go shopping for my younger brother and sister's birthday presents. Billy and Tish are nine and eleven this week, so Mom and I are making our annual trek for gifts. It would be great if Mom and I had some one-on-one time together that didn't revolve around my brother and sister, but we never do. So I take advantage of being in the car alone with her, not having to fight for the front seat.

"We have three hours and twenty-five minutes before the mall closes," I say. "Except for Sears; they're open until ten."

"We have plenty of time." My mother smiles.

Mom's real name is Mildred, but my grandfather calls her Dilly. "Dilly" makes my mother sound young and silly, which she isn't. She works hard running a day care business in our home. I've gotten used to the plastic slides and wheelbarrows all over the yard, even though I outgrew that stuff a long time ago. Sometimes when Tish and I come home from school, we help Mom play with the kids. It's like having six extra little brothers and sisters, which isn't always a good thing.

We pass a dead possum in the road; I bless myself three times, then roll up the window so the deadness won't come in.

As we take the exit, Mom asks me how Justin is doing. He's the four-year-old I baby-sit for a few afternoons a week. He has long, curly blond hair and people sometimes think he's a girl. He has this peculiar habit of running around naked. One day last week, I took him to the video store near his house. While I was paying for the video, a woman started yelling. I thought maybe the store was showing horror movies on the monitor, but when I turned around, Justin was standing in the center of the store with no clothes on. (At least he's not messy—his T-shirt and jeans were in a neat pile in the comedy section.) He can be a lot of trouble, but I love him so much, I'd baby-sit for free. Almost.

"I've saved up thirty dollars from baby-sitting. I should be able to find something for Billy and Tish tonight," I tell Mom.

There's a little red piece of paper sticking out of the glove compartment and I try not to stare at it as we drive.

It's probably just the cover of the service manual or a flyer from some store. But the little red tab taunts me, waves at me like a flag. I tell myself to ignore it and work on some puzzles instead. Why is *abbreviated* such a long word? Why does *monosyllabic* have five syllables? Why is it that when a door is open, it's *ajar*, but when a jar is open, it's not *adoor*?

My mother names every group singing on the oldies station—The Monkees, Herman's Hermits, The Turtles. But I'm not really listening. Every few minutes, I poke at the red paper with my finger or sneaker, trying to shove it back into the glove compartment. In the middle of the song "Do You Believe in Magic?" I can't stand it anymore and open the door to the glove box. The entire contents spill over onto my feet.

"Monica, what are you doing? You know that thing is a mess."

I pick up all the papers until I find the offender. "Aha!" I say. "A parking ticket."

My mother shrugs. "Probably your father's. Just shove it all back in there."

"But don't you have to pay them? What will happen if you don't?" *Suppose they come and take the car away, and Dad can't go to work anymore, so he gets fired, and we all have to move in with Grandpa, and we can't afford another car for years, and . . .*

I haven't said any of these possibilities out loud, but I can tell my mother's getting annoyed anyway because the lines around her mouth grow deep as trenches. I put the papers back and keep quiet while she parks the car. I tell myself the episode doesn't count as obsessing and I do the silent erasing routine I've done for years. I rap my knuckles on the armrest. *THIS does not count. This DOES not count. This does NOT count. This does not COUNT.* It's a superstitious chant, but in my mind the slate erases clean. The vow is still on.

We head into the mall. Filene's has a sale on jackets, so Mom buys one for both Tish and Billy. In the back of the store, almost shoved under a display, I find two beanbag chairs. One blue, one red. (Almost the same shade red as the parking ticket.)

"Tish and Billy will love these," I say. We check the tags to see if they're affordable. They've been marked down three times, so they are.

"Perfect for watching TV," Mom says as she helps me throw them in the cart.

We stop at Friendly's after shopping. As we eat our ice-cream cones I congratulate myself on keeping my pact: I had a mild setback earlier in the car, but the evening has gone well. Of course the sports announcer in my head still gives a play-by-play. *My mother's got a piece of walnut on her lip. Does she like being out alone with me or does she wish the whole family were here? Does she think I'm being funny and spontaneous or is she going to tell me to relax again?*

On the way home I realize that Billy and Tish won't be home from my grandfather's for another hour. I look forward to hanging out with Mom. But when I take the beanbags out of the car, they look lopsided. I hold one in each hand, weighing them like the scales of justice.

"The blue one is heavier." I hold them out to my mother to see for herself.

"They seem fine to me," she answers.

Jethro, our golden retriever, jumps up as we enter the house. I put the beanbags down and rub his ears. The normal thing to do would be to hang out with Jethro and Mom, but that itchy piece of my brain is on a mission and I realize my vow is history.

Because of the day care business, our house is filled with jars and crates and drawers with labels like CRAYONS, BEADS, and GAMES. I like how organized things are; what I don't like is the mess. Wax stuck to tables, sticky juice on the floor, loose feathers and glitter on the counter. My mother cleans every night so the house is presentable when people bring their kids the next morning. Needless to say, on weekends the house is a disaster area.

I drag both blobs to the bathroom and put them on the scale one at a time. "See, Mom, told you. The blue one weighs a little more."

"Monica, why don't you just relax? Let's go sit on the porch before Billy and Tish come home."

But my mind is made up. I unzip the two bags and take out the cotton pillow shapes underneath. My plan is to rip open the seam with scissors and spoon some of the stuffing from the blue one into the red one until they're equal.

My mother shakes her head. "I'm not staying around to help you."

A voice inside me tells me the bags are fine, that Billy and Tish will never notice the difference, that I need to keep my vow. But that voice is a tiny, squeaky one. The voice I hear most of the time, the sports announcer, tells me this is a problem and problems need to be fixed.

I carefully undo the stitches on each bag. Inside are white Styrofoam balls, like the peanuts they pack boxes with, only much smaller, what I imagine BBs look like. Jethro leans in, as if the sacks might contain a squirrel or rabbit. With the kitchen ladle, I spoon some of the stuffing from the blue one to the red. I'm surprised at how staticky they are. Soon my arms, the ladle, and the bathroom floor are covered with little white balls.

My mother's expression seems sad as she walks by. "Haven't we talked about being obsessive? How it isn't helpful?"

Only about fifty million times, I think. The fact that I broke the agreement with myself only adds to my growing anger.

My mother looks toward the driveway. "Billy and Tish are home." I check my watch. "They're thirteen minutes early." I rush to close up the bags, but my arms are still covered with the Styrofoam. Even worse, they have stuck to Jethro's hair like magnets. Tears cloud my vision. "Can you help me?"

"Monica, this is what happens when you try to make

everything be so perfect." When she leaves the bathroom to greet them, I slam the door shut. Soon I hear Billy and Tish in the kitchen.

Billy makes up for lost time by starting in early. "What's the matter, Monica? Need your privacy?"

Jethro barks when he hears Billy's voice. "Don't come in!" I holler. "I'm wrapping your birthday presents."

"What did you get me, a snowmobile? It looks like an avalanche out here."

It's impossible to imagine that Billy was once as cute and adorable as Justin. Now he has more in common with aliens on television than with me. Maybe he has some of Dad's acting genes, because he acts as if he's onstage twenty-four hours a day and the world is his audience. (To be fair, sometimes he is pretty funny; right now is *not* one of those times.)

"Enough of this nonsense," my mother says. "I'm opening the door."

"NO!" I run to stop her and as I do, I slip on the red bag. When the door opens, thousands of white pellets ricochet into the hall. So does Jethro, a polka-dot mess of furry Styrofoam.

"Surf's up!" Billy yells, pretending to ride a wave. He hugs Jethro, then recoils in horror. "My dog has turned into the Abominable Snowman. Run for your lives!" He scrambles into the kitchen with Jethro, leaving a slippery dusting in their wake.

I feel as if my body is encased in a straitjacket.

Tish gets the broom and begins to sweep up the mess. She's the poster child for a "normal" fifth-grade girl—she loves horses and ballerinas and sleep overs. Tish can braid her hair a hundred different ways, and she's usually pretty happy and uncomplicated. Half the time, I'm insanely jealous of her.

But right now, her pleasantness is welcome. "They're nice chairs," she says. "We can just fill them back up again."

I go to my room, disgusted with my failure. My mother follows.

"The bags were fine the way they were," she says.

"Not for me, they weren't."

"Now they're half the size. We'll be vacuuming for weeks and we'll never get all those beads up."

"I'll fix them tomorrow after school. You'll see. They'll be just as good as new."

"I don't know where you get this from, Monica." My mother seems more sad than angry. "God knows I don't have the time to make everything perfect."

I want to tell my mother that every time I looked at those beanbag chairs, I would have known they were uneven and it would have bothered me. Relentlessly. But how can she understand? She *never* cares about the details. If she had a Native American name it would be She-who-wears-two-unmatched-socks-without-noticing.

I lie awake long after the rest of them go to bed. My mind churns—maybe I should have picked the green chair instead, maybe the metal ladle made things more staticky, or maybe, just maybe, I should have left the bags alone. I try to concentrate on something else, like how boring Ms. Emerson is or what a dope Joey DeSalvo can be. Or how my wallpaper doesn't match. Dad put it up last year, and on the wall next to my closet, the daisies don't line up. Four of them have two centers like some kind of floral mutants. I pull the covers over my head and try to sleep.

Around one-fifteen, I get up to go to the bathroom. The beanbag chairs sit in the tub like two colorful beached whales, dragging themselves onshore to die.

When I show Lynn the beanbag chairs after school, she laughs so hard, she has to sit on the edge of the tub to catch her breath. "Monica, how do you *think* of these things?" Lynn would never take the time to measure two beanbags, shoveling their innards back and forth like stuffing in a Thanksgiving turkey. Never in a million years.

Lynn has lived across the street from me since we were little. Looking at the two of us, you wouldn't think we were best friends. She has three holes in each ear and wears silver rings on all her fingers—thumbs included. Her scrunchie is never in her hair, always on her wrist like a colorful cotton bracelet. She's funny and smart and fearless; I guess we have smart in common.

Lynn picks up a handful of pellets and throws them over our heads like snow or confetti. I want to tell her she's making even more of a mess, but she looks so ridiculous that I eventually end up laughing too. She climbs into the tub and lounges on the blue beanbag, kicking the red one up to the ceiling with both feet. I throw a handful of Styrofoam at her, and we laugh until my mother arrives in the hall with two dustpans. Even cleaning up is fun with Lynn.

After we finish, Lynn hands me a magazine as we head outside. It's one of the women's magazines Lynn continually swipes from her sister. Inside is a fashion spread of women wearing kilts. "What do you think? Is Bedford Junior High just waiting for us to start this trend?" Lynn's adventurous spirit even spills over into the area of clothes. Today she wears her mother's surgical scrub pants with three different layers of shirts.

I check out the model on the cover. "I'm not really sure about a kilt. . . ." But something besides the plaid skirt catches my attention. This month's quiz is titled **"Are You Obsessing?"** I wait until Lynn is concentrating on Jethro, then quickly skim the table of contents. Lynn and I have taken these quizzes before—**Does He Really Love You? Does Your Self-esteem Need a Boost?**—but maybe this will be the first one that is actually helpful. I even wonder if the obsession quiz is the reason Lynn brought over the magazine in the first place, some subtle hint for me to change. But she is rubbing Jethro's ears, talking baby talk to him, completely oblivious.

"Maybe we *should* start a kilt trend," I say. "Let me look through this. I'll give it back to you tomorrow."

After Lynn leaves, I run into my room and take the quiz. **Do you often think about what you "should have" said days after the fact?**

Try years.

Do you often find yourself not enjoying the present situation because your mind is stuck on something in the past?

Sorry, I can't answer the question; I'm too busy thinking about the time two years ago when I almost dropped Justin off the changing table.

Do you worry about social events before you attend them?

Only if you count getting ready for school, the bus stop, classes, homework, and dinner as social events.

I score a disgusting 9 out of 10, saved from 100 percent obsession because I don't obsess over "him." (Of course the reason I don't obsess over a guy is that I'm too busy obsessing about myself to have any time left over. Priorities, after all.)

I write down the quiz's four Helpful Hints in my notebook and soon have a list of techniques guaranteed to help me stop obsessing. No more measuring beanbag chairs for me. From here on in, it's freewheeling, spontaneous, unplugged Monica. I feel energized and do a few word games before dinner. Just for fun.

Because I feel like it. There, better already.

A LOST CHEF OIL

becomes

AISLE OF CLOTH

becomes

A FLESH TO COIL

becomes

IF SO, A COT HELL

becomes

ACHILLES' FOOT

becomes

LIFE AT SCHOOL

Helpful Hint #1 is a lame one—**Don't Worry About What Other People Think**.

Completely impossible. For anyone.

Still, I repeat the phrase like a mantra over and over on the way to English until Lynn stops me in the hall. She's wearing her old plaid Catholic school uniform. "It's not a kilt, but it's close," she says. Then she twirls around for me to see.

With her work boots and ankle socks as part of the ensemble, it actually looks good. Lynn is definitely not worried about what other people think.

"Hey, I've got a word game even *you* can't figure out," she says. "I found it in the newspaper this morning."

"Let's hear it."

"Name an eight-letter word with only one vowel."

Hmmm. I wish I had my Scrabble tiles to help me with this one. "Only one vowel for eight letters?" I ask.

We take our seats in Mr. Bergeron's class. "Yes, and it's not a weird word either. A totally normal word." She takes a penny from her purse. "Heads you get it, tails you don't."

"I'll get it," I reassure her.

Mr. Bergeron is late, and by the time he apologizes his way into the room, I've already figured it out. I lean toward Lynn and whisper, *"Strength."*

She hits my arm. "Do you have a dictionary in your brain?"

"Strengths is even better," I say. "That's nine letters with one vowel."

Lynn shakes her head and tosses her penny back in her purse. "I give up," she quips.

I settle down into a wonderful nonobsessive day.

Before the quiz, Mr. Bergeron reviews oxymorons— phrases of two opposite words paired up to make something new. The phrase makes sense until you actually look at the two words and see how opposite they really are. He gives us some examples like *jumbo shrimp*, *pretty ugly*, and *computer jock*.

Lynn passes me a piece of paper. It says: *Loose tights. How's* that *for an oxymoron?* She has drawn a picture of a girl with baggy leggings down around her ankles. I laugh so hard, I snort quickly. I cover my mouth, totally embarrassed by my outburst.

Christine Franklin, two rows over, scrawls a note on a piece of paper and passes it across the aisle to Joey. A feeling of dread hits me in the stomach as everyone sitting between them opens the note and reads it before passing it along. Lynn thinks Christine resents me because she used to be the smartest kid in her old school and now she's just the second smartest. I think there must have been a sign hanging in the hall when Christine transferred this year that said, NOW HIRING—POSITION AVAILABLE TO TORTURE AND HUMILIATE EIGHTH-GRADE STUDENT MONICA DEVON. NO EXPERIENCE NECESSARY, INQUIRE WITHIN. I peek into my notebook and read today's magazine tip again, hoping it will help.

When Joey gets the note, he holds it up so everyone around us can read it too. It says: *Here's an oxymoron for Monica—BUTT HEAD.*

I slink down into my seat.

Lynn leans toward me and whispers, "Christine's not worth a second of your time. She's such a moron. Such an oxy."

I almost laugh at Lynn's new joke, but laughter is what got Christine started on me in the first place. I know Lynn's and the magazine's advice is good, but I also know I will rewind this episode a thousand times in the sicko VCR of my mind. Maybe the letters in Lynn's name saved her—that since LYNN can't be rearranged into anything else, she's destined to a simple, easy life, without complications. I, on the other hand, have IN COMA to deal with, among other things.

Mr. Bergeron hands out the tests to the first person in every row.

I don't know why I worry—after playing word games with Grandpa all these years, I could take the test with my brain tied behind my back. It's a good thing too, because my brain is busy anyway, thinking about Christine and her stupid note.

I finish the test early and spend the rest of the time working on a new anagram. I try to wipe out the day the way Mr. Bergeron erases the board. *THIS does not count. This DOES not count. This does NOT count. This does not COUNT.*

After class, Christine waltzes by my desk and smirks. I smile and point to her cotton blouse. "Christine," I say. "Nice shirt." She gives me a look like I just asked her for twenty dollars, then shakes her head and walks away.

I try to control my grin. And she thinks she's so smart! CHRISTINE—NICE SHIRT. Too bad *that* anagram wasn't on the test.

I should feel good—I one-upped Christine *and* aced the quiz. But still . . . this all-too-familiar feeling of dread is lodged somewhere between my stomach and my heart. This feeling that no matter what happens in my life, I'll always feel a little outside, a little off center. More than anything, I want to feel alive, I want to stop worrying and obsessing about being wrong. I guess deep down, what I really want is to feel like someone else. When the bell rings for class, I hurry to the door. (Never first, never last, always in the middle.) I am mortified when Mr. Bergeron asks to see me.

"Monica, you've been a whiz with those anagrams all

week." He leans against his desk and smiles. "Have you been doing them for a long time?"

"I've been doing them with my grandfather for years," I answer. "He doesn't even have to use paper. He does them in his head."

"He sounds awesome," Mr. Bergeron says, and I cringe at him trying to be cool. It's like the ties he wears, always filled with pool cues, bowling pins, and rolling dice. So different from Mr. Bergeron himself. It's like his neck has this secret life, taking chances and risks while the rest of him coughs quietly into his hand and fiddles with his glasses. Mr. Bergeron is reliable in a world of constant change.

"Constant change," I say. "That's an oxymoron you could have had on the quiz."

"It certainly is." He tilts his head to look at me. "Keep up the good work, Monica."

He doesn't realize I have no choice.

On the way out of the room, I wonder if I should be glad Mr. Bergeron is happy with me or if I shouldn't care about his opinion because that's worrying about what other people think of me. It's a catch-22 situation that I think about all the way to Spanish, where I resume the real work of the day—obsessing about Christine.

I FLEE A MOTH

becomes

A HEEL OF TIM

becomes

I HOT FEMALE

becomes

HEAL ME OF IT

becomes

A HOLE ME FIT

becomes

LIFE AT HOME

The second Helpful Hint from the magazine quiz is— **Be With Loved Ones. Take Advantage of Their Support.** Dad came back from his business trip last night, so we'll all be together today and I can see if this tip works. My father goes away on business about once a month, and every time he goes, he brings back gifts just like he did when we were little. This time he went to Seattle, and he brought us back little flashlights shaped like salmon. My mother tells him not to waste his money on airport trinkets. But we always make a big deal out of them, usually because we're just happy to have him home.

Dad tried for many years to be an actor full-time, but now he sells telemarketing software to companies that call you at dinnertime and bug you to buy stuff. His heart really belongs to the theater, though, and sometimes he has an annoying habit of talking in this overacting Shakespeare voice that drives the rest of us crazy.

Mom serves turkey meat loaf tonight and Dad comments at least ten times that you can't tell it's not real meat loaf. He talks about the play he's starring in at the Community Theatre next month. He's got the lead in *Death of a*

Salesman, which he says is the role of a lifetime. Tish asks him if the salesman dies in the end, but Dad tells her she'll have to come to the play to find out. *Suppose this part makes him realize how much he hates his sales job, and he quits and starts doing commercials for local grocery stores, and he has to dress up like a hot dog in Stop & Shop, and the entire eighth grade sees him and makes fun of me, and . . .*

I lasso my mind like a runaway stallion—whoa!

After dinner we all play Monopoly. My mother won't let me be the banker because she says it's what I do to avoid losing. So I choose the shoe and wait for my turn.

It's hard to enjoy playing with Billy because he usually just takes the race car and smashes it into every house and hotel on the board. I line up my money in piles, starting with the ones, moving up to the five hundreds.

After playing for a while, I land on Pennsylvania Avenue, which has a hotel.

"Pay up!" Billy says.

"You don't have a hotel there," I say.

"Sure, I do. You see it, don't you?"

"You just put that there. You didn't buy it."

"Of course I did."

"Mom?"

She looks up from her checkbook, which she balances when it's not her turn. "I don't know, honey."

"Dad?" I try not to sound like I'm begging.

"William, did ye or did ye not acquire that hotel by legal means?"

Oh, brother.

"I *did* buy it," Billy says. "Not last turn, but the turn before, remember?"

My father shrugs and points to my neat stacks of money. "Perhaps the young maiden doth pay her precious sibling."

"No!" I shout. This is one of those times I absolutely, completely, totally detest being the oldest. It is also one of those times I absolutely, completely, totally detest being a girl. Billy gets away with things Tish and I would never dream of.

"It's not fair!" I yell. "And stop talking like that!"

Thankfully, Tish takes my side. "I don't think he bought that hotel."

"I got that hotel free from owning all three greens," Billy hollers. "That's the way Gus and I play."

I hold up the cover of the box. "We're playing by *these* rules, not ones you make up because you feel like it."

"And what are rules meant to be?" Billy asks.

"NOT BROKEN," I answer. I take my money and leave the table. "I'm not playing with cheaters."

"Okay, Billy. Cut Monica some slack," my mother says.

My father gives me a look like I am ruining all his fun.

"Don't say it like that, like I'm some kind of baby. He's wrong!" So much for family support. I begin to wonder if it's a good idea to get advice from a women's magazine.

Billy throws the hotel back into the box. "Okay, fine."

Tish takes the die and rolls.

The game has lost most of its fun, but we keep playing anyway. Billy tells Dad about the contest he, Andy, and Gus had jumping off the garage roof into the bushes, and Tish tells Dad she is singing a solo in the end-of-the-year concert. I tell him about Mr. Bergeron's class and how I made up lots of new anagrams and oxymorons. In the middle of talking, I notice Billy scooping gravy from the bowl and dribbling it down his chin.

"Gross!" Tish laughs. She throws her $500 bills at him for emphasis.

"Enough, enough," my mother says.

No one listens to her either, because Dad takes his money and throws it at Billy too. Then Billy takes all the money from the table and tosses it into the air.

My father jumps up from his chair, and before long he's chasing Billy and Tish around the kitchen. Mom just shakes her head, tired but not really mad.

I want to tell them that what I was saying was important—to me at least. That I liked learning these new things. Besides that, I was ahead and in a few minutes I would have won the game. But I know if I tell them how I feel, I'll be reprimanded for "taking things too seriously" or "not going with the flow"—whatever *that* means. So I do what I do most of the time, choose a response that won't irritate anybody. **Be With Loved Ones.** Am I the only person these helpful hints didn't work for? Probably . . .

I race down the hall after Billy and Tish. And when Mom joins in and tackles us one by one, I fall to the floor, willingly.

Back in my room later, I lie on the bed and listen to the muffled sounds of Billy and Tish in the next room. I like it this way. They're home, but I don't have to deal with them. Sometimes I don't feel related—a misfit in my own family. A family outsider—I guess that's an oxymoron too.

I take out my kaleidoscope from the bottom drawer of my desk. I stare into the eyepiece, turning the focus wheel slowly, watching the pieces drop into place. The big wheel of color is broken down into smaller wheels, and inside each of those circles are more wheels. Some kaleidoscopes use bits of plastic for color. When Grandpa gave me this one for Christmas two years ago, he said the inside was made of glass. The wheel changes from turquoise to lime to slate, from a daisy to a dinner plate to a royal crest.

It's the changing I love, how easy it is. First this—slight turn—then that. No big decisions. No hemming and hawing, as my mom would say. Why can't *I* change that easily?

I am determined to find a way to stop obsessing. If the Helpful Hints don't work, I'll find another way.

Whenever my grandpa comes to visit, he brings tools and materials for us to make things. Tish and Billy are not as close to our grandfather as I am; they usually prefer to play outside—today they plan to explore the cemetery. Billy asks if I feel like going. Part of me wants to run through the woods like a cheetah, fierce and fast, tearing through leaves and branches. (It's an image I long to be, but it's so different from who I am. CHEETAH—THE ACHE.) Another part of me wants to cover my head with a blanket and wait for Billy and Tish to leave. They're connected by some kind of spontaneous, fearless gene that didn't get passed on to me. When I tell him no, Billy shakes his head, probably wondering why he bothered to ask me in the first place. There's just no way for him to know that for me, the cheetah never wins.

When Grandpa finally arrives, we head to the basement. It's the perfect day to follow Helpful Hint #3: **Keep Busy.** The article mentioned exercising, vacuuming, and baking, but I'm sure craft projects qualify.

I like to work alongside my grandpa, smell his pine soap scent, watch his eyes squint over his scratchy glasses. He takes out the tiny brass tools he used as a jeweler when he worked in Harvard Square. He doesn't fix watches anymore; he makes little projects and sculptures out of things he finds—wood, shells, old candlestick holders.

He unfolds the worn canvas flap by flap, revealing the tiny brass hammer, the three pairs of tweezers, and the wire cutter with the worn ends. Then he hands me a few thin pieces of wood from the box.

"Let's see what you can do today," he says.

I search through the box. "Where are the instructions we used last time?"

"Improvise," Grandpa says as he closes the lid.

"But I don't want to." I open up the box again and take out the instructions for the picture frame we made last week.

"Okay," he concedes. "We'll follow the directions again."

I spread out the folded sheet in front of us and we work in silence for a long while. I like being next to him, like the ticking of his old-fashioned watch, even the bits of dandruff on his green cardigan sweater.

I mention the oxymorons I've been working on—*exact estimate*, *definite maybe*, and *soft rock*.

"I've got an oxymoron for you," he says. "It's a part of history I lived through. When I couldn't find a job and learned to fix watches."

I think for a few moments; I know better than to ask my grandpa for hints. After a few minutes I come up with the answer. "Great Depression."

He smiles. "Nothing great about it. I'll vouch for that."

We work in silence for a while; this is one of the best things about being with him. After one of his visits, the rest of the world always seems so noisy and loud. I know that sooner or later he will begin our game, and after a few minutes, he does.

"We'll start with an easy one," he says. "ANGERED."

I try to scramble the letters around in my mind, but I soon run to the desk for a pen. I mix the letters around as if they are magnets on a refrigerator.

"GARDEN?" I ask, but I know as soon as I say it that it's wrong.

He shakes his head no, still hammering the wire to the board. "You're missing an *e*."

I get mad at myself for rushing and making a stupid mistake. I continue to cross the letters out until I finally come up with a correct anagram.

"ANGERED. ENRAGED," I say. "That's a good one— they mean the same thing."

"Synonyms," he says. "I thought you'd like that." He pounds the small brass nails with the precision of a diamond cutter.

"I have one for you." I've been saving this one since Mr. Bergeron's class. "FUNERAL. Two words. And the answer is kind of funny."

He doesn't need a pen. Or much time, for that matter. His mind just works that way, paying attention to new information whether it's jumbled or not.

"FUNERAL," he repeats. "Well, I suppose it could be FLEA URN, but you didn't say it was a cremation for insects."

I can tell he enjoys building up to the answer, so I let him.

"And I doubt it's LEAN FUR," he continues. "So it must be REAL FUN."

I bow down to him and applaud.

His smile tells me he enjoyed the puzzle. "I'll have to tell my buddies at the coffee shop about that one."

We go back and forth between silence and playing the game until we are done with our projects. One of the nails on the bottom of my frame isn't flush. I hammer it down again, then hold it up for him to see.

"Very good," he says. "But you already know how to make a frame like that."

"I know. I like it." I try not to sound defensive.

"Next time we'll do a new project, okay? No instructions."

"Sure," I say. "Sounds great." What it actually sounds like is one of those subjective essays Mr. Bergeron gives us to increase our creativity.

As I sweep up the small bits of wood from the table, Grandpa kisses the top of my head. "I've got a surprise for you." He sits in the chair solemnly, then leans toward me and whispers, "I want you to have this." He hands me a box.

"Grandpa, it's not my birthday," I say.

"Of course not. Your birthday isn't till November. Do I need a birthday to give my Monica a present?"

Inside the box is a worn cloth envelope folded into

thirds—a smaller version of his own tool kit. I unwrap the cloth carefully. Inside are a tiny brass hammer, two pairs of tweezers, a wire cutter, and a pair of pliers.

"I haven't used these in thirty or forty years." He picks up the wire cutter. "Cleaned and sharpened them yesterday. They're working fine." He puts a piece of wire between the blades of the cutter and—*snap*—the tool neatly cuts the wire in half.

"They're beautiful," I say. "I'll take extra-special care of them, I promise." I plan to put it in the bottom drawer of my desk, next to my kaleidoscope.

He hands me a box full of wire and wood. "See what you can come up with." He pauses. "No instructions."

I'm making progress, I think. Today I kept busy; my mind didn't wander to Monday's test, or Christine Franklin, or the pile of green olives I poked out of the olive loaf at lunch. Maybe this magazine is on to something after all.

I put the tools inside the box of wood and run upstairs. I love that they're mine and not a present for all three of us. But Grandpa doesn't know me well enough if he thinks I'm going to make anything without a blueprint.

It's not just a problem for making crafts; it's one of life's major flaws. There really should be an instruction manual.

On the way home from school, I stop by Justin's house. I don't have to baby-sit, but it's a blistering afternoon and I can practice my final Helpful Hint—**Be Spontaneous.** It'll be easy to be spontaneous with Justin's mother, Darcy.

Darcy—she won't let me call her Ms. Travers—has long blond hair that's never combed. It's usually falling out of a pair of chopsticks, or when she can't find those, a couple of chewed-up pencils. Her hair never looks messy, though, just casually elegant, as my mother would say (yet another oxymoron to add to my list). Darcy is a guidance counselor at the high school, but because of cutbacks, she only works part-time. She also paints—lots of rain forest stuff—and her fingers and arms are usually splattered with bright colors, a palette of pastel freckles. When I baby-sit on Tuesday or Thursday afternoons, she paints on canvases in the basement with a Walkman on and the windows wide open.

Justin rushes down the swing set slide in his bathing suit. "Geronimo!" It's still only late spring, but that doesn't seem to stop him. Justin pours some vegetable oil down the length of the slide to make it slippery and fast. Darcy takes a turn behind him, screaming with laughter.

I watch them laughing from the sidelines, a place where I seem to have purchased season tickets. When Darcy sees me, she hoses herself off, then holds out the hose so Justin and I can take a drink.

"Your turn, Monica." She points to the slide.

"Darcy, I'm in my school clothes."

"I'm sure we've got something that'll fit." She eyes one of her shirts on the clothesline.

"No, that's okay," I say. But when I remember what today's mission is, I trudge inside and change into Darcy's old Grateful Dead T-shirt and shorts.

Justin greases up the slide and I fall to the bottom with a thud. "Yes, yes," Justin cries. "More!" The three of us take turns on the slide until we're exhausted.

"Hey," Darcy says. "I read something about a craft fair at the junior high. Have you thought about entering anything? Those picture frames?" She rubs the oil into her legs, then props them on the picnic table to get some sun.

"Oh no," I answer. "I just make them for me."

"Of course," she says. "Why does anybody do anything?"

I try to decide if that's really true, but before I can think about it, I catch Justin sneaking toward me with the hose. I hop out of the way just in time. (JUSTIN—JUST IN TIME.) He decides against chasing me and begins to water the sandbox instead. Darcy watches the sand spill onto the grass in a frothy mess without saying a word. Then she jumps up and runs to the back door.

"I just remembered something," she says. She hurries inside, returning a few minutes later with a beach cooler. I assume she's bringing out a snack, but no. The cooler is packed to the brim with snowballs.

"Justin and I made these in March." She holds one up for my inspection. "The basement freezer is full of them."

We divide them into three piles, then set up lawn chairs as barricades. Justin lobs one over my chair, hitting me squarely on the shoulder. We throw them at each other with speed—a five-minute battle that leaves us laughing hysterically. I watch Darcy chasing Justin through the yard and wonder how someone wearing a bathing suit and throwing snowballs can counsel high school kids. But I figure that quality is one reason she's so good at her job. Last year, the students gathered almost a thousand signatures on a petition so she wouldn't be laid off. It's why I keep dropping by all the time too—partly to see Justin, but partly to see if Darcy's free spirit can rub off on me.

Justin leisurely holds on to his last snowball, taking little licks every few minutes. I tell him to stop, especially after the meningitis scare at our school a few months ago.

"No one put their germs on these," Darcy says. "I used fresh snow. They're fine."

But the germs from the ground, the mittens, the freezer, and the cooler fill my mind like nasty amoebas. *What if Justin gets sick, really sick? What if he does get meningitis and*

Darcy has to rush him to the hospital and he has to stay on an IV all week and anybody who came in contact with him has to go on antibiotics and . . . I tell myself to calm down. I'm overreacting again. He's not going to get meningitis. Today's lesson is be spontaneous, not imagine the worst-possible situation in the world. But the thought of the infected snow freezes my new spirit; with every bite Justin takes, I feel my body tighten. Soon I change back into my school clothes and get ready to leave. So much for being spontaneous.

"Are you okay?" Darcy asks. "You're not worried about that snow, are you?"

I assure her I'm not. She doesn't buy it.

She pulls me close to her. "Save your energy for things that are *worth* worrying about," she says. "Like the environment."

I worry about the environment all the time. Especially my mental one.

When I get back home, I climb into bed and doodle all over the list in my notebook. I rearrange the letters to HELPFUL HINTS. FLESH LIP HUNT. HE'LL SHIFT PUN. PULL HEN SHIFT. Hey, you magazine editors—thanks for the great advice. Looks like I'm back to where I started, Ms. 98.762 percent obsessing.

I suppose I should be happy it's not 100 percent.

Maybe my next idea shouldn't rely on a magazine quiz. Maybe I should try something normal, like asking Mom for help or talking to Darcy. But the thought of either of these choices makes me crouch even further under the covers.

I flip through my notebook, a written account of the blips of my mind. If only life were an anagram and I could throw the pieces of myself in the air, high into the sky, and when they came down, I could rearrange them into something the same yet different. Monica but not Monica.

That's not too much to ask for, is it?

Lynn and I are playing games after dinner. We started with Mancala and are now in the middle of Scrabble. To say that I am killing Lynn is an understatement. (The score is 543 to 217.)

Lynn presses the fast-forward button on the tape player, then pauses with concentration. After a few seconds, she hits stop, then play. When the song cues up perfectly, she looks at me and smiles.

"Do you think Mr. Bergeron is dating Miss Cotter?" For Lynn, the most interesting subjects in school are advanced gossip and love interest speculation.

"Hello? He's married," I answer. I add MENT to ASSIGN and score an easy twenty-six points. A double-word score. Thank you very much.

"I know, but I saw them walking down the hall twice this week and he was laughing both times. Not just laughing. *Really* laughing." She adds an S to CLOCK for fourteen.

"Maybe she's a comedian and she was practicing her routine on him."

"Yeah, I bet *Mrs.* Bergeron would love to know what

Miss Cotter is practicing on her husband." Lynn kicks off her shoes and lies down on the rug. She looks at the board, bored. "Are we done?"

I nod, used to Lynn giving up after only twenty minutes. She's rubbing Jethro's ears and staring up at the ceiling fan. I lie on the floor next to her and scratch his belly.

Most of our conversations are based on superficial things—classes, TV, living on the same street. It would be safe to keep things light and breezy. But I need advice so badly, I take advantage of the moment to ask her a difficult question.

"Do you ever wish you were different?" I ask.

"What do you mean?" Her eyes continue to follow the fan.

I rephrase the question. "Do you ever think about being another kind of person? Like if you could be more generous or less complaining, that type of thing?"

Lynn sits up and shuts off the tape. "This is because I wouldn't lend Billy that video last week, right? Well, I didn't give it to him because every time I do, he wrecks—"

"NO!" I interrupt. "Not because of that. I used generous as an example."

"You don't think I'm a complainer, do you?"

"Oh, forget it."

Lynn continues to stroke Jethro's ears. A few minutes later she says, "I think I know what you mean."

I relax just a bit.

"I spend a lot of time thinking about that."

"Really?"

"But when it comes right down to it, I wouldn't want to be anyone else, would you?"

"Well, no, but . . ."

"You know what your problem is?" Lynn asks. "You think too much. Weighing beanbags, making up anagrams for Christine . . . You're my best friend, but admit it, sometimes you're a wacko."

"Sometimes *you're* a wacko," I reply.

"Yeah, but I don't spend half my life worrying about it."

(Try 98.762 percent. The conversation is obviously not going the way I planned.)

"You need a way to be more spontaneous," Lynn says.

"I had a snowball fight in May! You can't *get* any more spontaneous than that."

"You think if you spend your time worrying about every possible thing that can happen, you'll be protected," she says.

"That's ridiculous." I pause. "Protected from what?"

"From life, from mistakes, from being wrong."

"Everyone wants to save themselves from messing up," I say. "Not just me."

"Nobody else makes a full-time job out of it," she replies.

Across the street, the porch lights flash on and off, Lynn's father's signal for her to go home. Lynn sighs. "Heads I go, tails I stay and get my father pissed off." She sticks her hand in her pocket. "You got a penny?"

I check my pockets and the table.

"Never mind." Lynn grabs a facedown Scrabble tile from the box. "Vowel, I stay, consonant, I go." She turns the tile over. It's an R. "See ya."

She gathers up her tapes. "You're not mad at me, are you?"

"Of course not," I say halfheartedly.

"I know being so intense makes you unhappy some-times. I'm just trying to help."

"I know you are." I lean against the couch, more frus-trated than when I started.

Lynn yells good-bye to my parents and sprints back across the street.

What was I thinking—asking Lynn for advice like she actually might have some kind of miracle answer? I pick up the R and toss it from hand to hand. PHIL MYER'S WOMBAT—WHAT IS MY PROBLEM?

NIGHT MOSS FETISH

becomes

MEG TOSS THIN FISH

becomes

SHE FIGHT MOST SIN

becomes

GHOSTS INFEST HIM

becomes

MISS HIGHEST FONT

becomes

SOFT MESH INSIGHT

becomes

SOMETHING SHIFTS

After Lynn leaves, I grab a handful of Scrabble tiles and shake them up like the lottery Ping-Pong balls they show on TV. I feel comfortable because the letters are here.

I toss the tiles onto the rug and turn over the ones landing blank side up. Without the limitations of the board, I rearrange the tiles, making as many new words as possible. It's truly amazing—an H can be a part of *hunger*, part of *Buddha*, part of *chair*, part of *thyroid* . . . so many choices. Lynn probably thinks that people have that many choices every day, that being stuck into just one part of ourselves is a silly, narrow way to live. I wish there was a way to be spontaneous without being wrong. A way to be less in control, less worried about being perfect . . .

I pick out the tiles for the letters A, B, C, and D and shake them in my hand. Of course, if life were like one of Mr. Bergeron's multiple-choice tests, then one of these letters would *have* to represent the correct answer.

Here's an idea. What if these four letters represented choices in the *real* world, not answers on some English test? Suppose I pick an A; what would *that* choice be?

Hmmm. If I pick an A, I'll put away these games and get ready for bed. A—a nice safe choice. And if it's a B . . . I'll eat the leftover three-bean salad from dinner. (That's certainly more of a risk; I hate three-bean salad.) Picking a C means I volunteer to clean Billy's room. (I laugh out loud at the complete absurdity of that one.) And a D means . . . what a D usually means, in Mr. Bergeron's class—all of the above. I work out the logistics of D—I'll eat the three-bean salad, then clean Billy's room, then pick up the game and go to bed.

I place the tiles facedown on the board, nervous with excitement. I mix them up and take a deep breath. I pick the tile closest to the middle.

It's a C.

Boy, is Billy going to be surprised.

Part of me says, "This is ridiculous; do your homework, go to bed," but another part of me feels compelled to play. Maybe this is the ticket out of my head. I get up and walk down the hall to Billy's room.

"Get away, spastic stranger!" He points his laser gun at me and pretends to shoot. I ignore him and scan the room. Pigsty would be a compliment.

"I was just wondering if you wanted any help cleaning up?" I ask.

He jumps from the bed to a pile of clothes on the floor. "A mad predator has eaten my sister and is masquerading inside her body!" He continues to shoot.

"Billy, I'm serious. I'm worried your room might be giving Jethro fleas."

He holds the gun against my chest and leans in close. "What do you want, asteroid monkey?"

The situation strikes me as ridiculous—I am begging Billy to let me clean his room. Forget this dumb multiple-choice game. It was a stupid idea. I turn to leave, but something stops me. The part of me that likes all of life's loose ends to be tied, the part of me that likes every headband lined up on my bureau, that insists on playing Monopoly by the rules, that can't leave a word alone until it's been jumbled up a hundred times. The part of me that knows I can't leave the game half done.

I begin by sorting through the clothes on his floor and bed. Holding them at arm's length, I try to tell which ones are dirty and throw them in the hamper. The others I fold and put in drawers. Billy is too stunned to move when I ask him to get a rag from the kitchen, so I get one myself. I put icing on my performance by humming "Whistle While You Work."

Tish stares with Billy in equal amazement. "Are you being punished? What did you do—murder someone?" she asks.

I clean Billy's mirror and dust his bureau, then stack all his baseball caps inside one another on the top shelf of his closet.

"Just a little spring cleaning," I answer.

Before long, Mom pops her head in. "Good for you, Monica. Tish, why don't you get started on yours?"

"No way. My report on fungus is due," she says.

"Plenty of samples here," I shoot back.

My cheerfulness drives her from the room.

Mom tries to force Billy into helping me, but I insist on doing it myself. I finish half an hour later, exhausted.

"Thanks, Mon." Billy actually seems pleased. "Let me know when your fever goes down."

I chug a glass of juice and head back to the living room to put the Scrabble game away.

"I figured since you were helping Billy, I would help you." My mother hands me the box. "Nice job. I appreciate it."

She kisses the top of my head and I feel proud. It sometimes seems she loves me most when I'm doing something good—helping her with the day care kids, getting top grades. Maybe that's one of the reasons I try so hard to be perfect. But who knows? Maybe I try so hard just for me.

I collapse on my bed, open up the game, and search through all the tiles until I find the letters A, B, C, and D again. Then I go to the bottom of my desk and take out the box with my kaleidoscope. It's nestled inside a velvet bag. I gently remove it and place the kaleidoscope back in the cradle of the box. The four tiles fit nicely inside the bag; I can hear them rattle when I shake it. Luckily there are eight other A's, three other D's, and one B and C left in the game box, so they won't be missed. Of course, the two blank tiles could fill in for any of the missing letters. (Like anyone but me plays anyway.)

Boy, is Lynn in for a surprise. I decide to ask the letters if I should tell her about the Game. A and B are yes; C and D are no.

I slip my hand into the bag and pull out a tile. D. I can't tell Lynn about Multiple Choice as long as I play.

I lie on my bed in the dark, shaking my new velvet game. I'll keep the letters with me at all times and log my choices in my notebook.

I'VE FINALLY FOUND IT!

A way to be me . . . and not me.

The Ground Rules

- **A** is a normal choice, something I might do anyway.
- **B** is just plain dumb.
- **C** is mean, completely out of character.
- **D** is a charitable, sacrificial choice.
- One game per day.
- No backing out.
- I repeat, no backing out.
  I do what the letters say, no matter what.

Since I've taken the choice out of making a decision, whatever the letters dictate *is* the right choice, the only choice. The perfect choice.

It's so calming to know I can't be wrong anymore.

HO, ICICLE! MELT UP!

becomes

HECTIC PLUME OIL

becomes

I HEM UP LICE CLOT

becomes

I PITCH MOLECULE

becomes

UPHILL ICE COMET

becomes

MULTIPLE CHOICE

Choice #1—
What to Wear to School

A) Jeans and a T-shirt.

B) My pajamas.

C) The junior bridesmaid gown I wore to my cousin Marla's wedding that Tish has wrapped in fifty pounds of plastic to keep clean for her choir solo.

D) My old black pants—and I'll donate my new ones to the Salvation Army on the way home from school.

Here goes . . .

AM I OUT OF MY MIND?

I stare at the beige tile in my hand—B. I burrow deeper into the covers like a groundhog avoiding spring. I CAN'T WEAR PAJAMAS TO SCHOOL! Talk about fear and humiliation. . . . And the whole point of this stupid game is to liberate me. Liberate me straight into a padded room is more like it.

First of all, there are too many details. Mom certainly won't let me walk out the door in what I'm wearing. (Red cotton tops and bottoms with a cowboy-and-Indian motif, hand-me-downs from my cousin Timmy.) Of course, I could roll the pants up to my knees and wear my raincoat if I were going to do it, which I'm not. Although I suppose it's better than walking through the halls of Bedford Junior High in a peach-colored chiffon gown.

My mother yanks off the covers. "Monica, you're going to be late." She eyes the Scrabble tiles on the bed. "This is no time for games. Literally. Let's go. Bathroom's free." After she leaves, I pick up the four tiles and place them gently in the velvet bag. I stumble to the bathroom.

I can always tell her I'm feeling sick, that my stomach

hurts after all the vinegar in that stupid three-bean salad we had for dinner.

I stare at myself in the mirror. For as long as I can remember, I have been compulsive, obsessive—a perfectionist. I've spent hours, days, months being miserable for it. And it's only gotten worse. If I could think of another way to change, I would. Even if my percentage of obsessing time drops from 98.762 percent to 95.391 percent, it would be worth it. And right now this is the only option I've come up with. I've got to walk through the fear.

I brush my teeth, put on a barrette that matches the cactus on my pajamas, and get ready to go.

"Bye!" I pull the raincoat tight around me and reach up to give my mother a kiss. Mr. Coleman has just dropped off Peter, and Mom is pulling his sweatshirt over his head. She looks down at my bare legs under my coat.

"Are you wearing a skirt today?"

I try not to lie about what I'm doing. "No."

Luckily Peter starts screaming for an orange and Mom waves us off. Luck is also with me when Paula meets up with Tish and Billy to walk to the bus stop. I sit alone on the bus. The question is—what am I going to do once I get to school?

For the first time in my life, I am thinking on my feet. Which feels good for about thirty seconds. Then the usual terror begins.

I stand in front of my locker like a petrified tree. If I don't hurry up and take my raincoat off, I'll miss the final bell and I'll have to walk into class late, in front of everyone. On the other hand, I will soon be standing in the school corridor in my pajamas. When I see Mr. Bergeron walk into class, I know I have to hurry. I spin the dial to my locker three times.

You don't have to do this, a voice inside me says. It was funny at first, but now it's not. Say you're sick and go to the nurse's office. GO!

But I don't. I made a commitment to change my life, to live by a new set of rules. I'm going to do it. I hang my coat in my locker and walk into Mr. Bergeron's class.

The first person I see is Lynn. She grins from ear to ear. "Pajamas—excellent. Even better than a kilt."

Behind Lynn, Mike the Mosquito asks me if I want a pillow. Joey DeSalvo lifts his head from his desk for a moment, then puts it back down, oblivious.

Mr. Bergeron looks as if he might say something, but thankfully he doesn't. I try to concentrate on Mr. Bergeron's lesson in dangling participles without feeling conspicuous. But when Christine finally notices what I'm wearing, it becomes impossible. Suddenly she bursts out laughing while Mr. Bergeron writes on the board.

"Hey, Mr. Bergeron, is it okay if I come to school in my underwear tomorrow? I mean, since some of us are trying to get comfortable."

Several people laugh, and all eyes are glued on me. Maybe someone else could think of something witty and clever to say, but I just sit there like a mannequin modeling pajamas.

You don't have to be the same person anymore, I tell myself. You don't have to be mousy Monica who can't be wrong. You *can* take chances, you *can* be spontaneous. You *can* be someone who writes the rules, not just follows them. And best of all, you can be someone who doesn't obsess about what others think. Multiple Choice can change everything. Make up a response, pick a letter.

"Were you feeling sick this morning, Monica?" Mr. Bergeron asks.

I look down at the floor while I answer Mr. Bergeron. "I think pajamas should be the school uniform," I answer. "Half these classes are so boring, we *should* be wearing sleepwear."

Lynn bursts out laughing, along with several others. Even Christine and Joey smile.

"But not this class, Mr. Bergeron," I add. "This class is very interesting."

The poor guy looks puzzled, probably wondering why his best student has suddenly gone psycho on him. He fiddles with his glasses, then turns back to the board.

I spend half the morning giggling to myself and the other half worried that Mr. Bergeron will hate me forever. I can't believe those words came out of my mouth. For a minute there I almost sounded like Lynn.

I race out the door—second, not first—before Mr.

Bergeron can grab me. By third period, I am used to the looks in the hall. I never realized how much I blended into the tile before. Lynn catches up to me going into Ms. Hodgett's class.

"I love it, Mon, but are you okay? I couldn't believe you said that to Mr. Bergeron."

Of course, I couldn't believe it either, but I reassure Lynn that I'm fine. Later, when Ms. Hodgett sends me to the nurse, insisting I must have a fever, I reassure both of them too. For some strange reason, I revel in my newfound control. On the way home I don't obsess, I don't play a million what-if's. I cross my arms over my chest and look out the window of the bus, enjoying my new power.

Luckily when I get home, Mom is in the backyard with Melissa, Peter, and Charlie and I have a chance to change before I see her. I fold my pajamas neatly under my pillow and plop down on the bed. I made it through the day. I made it through a humiliating, exhilarating, scary, new day. I tell myself I can back out now, that making it through today was a victory in and of itself, and that I don't have to go one step further in Multiple Choice if I don't want to.

But I do.

When I run out to the backyard, I can almost feel the cheetah.

I'M

THE WORLD

(I'm on top of the world!)

I spend the next several days selecting choices that are out of character but not as wacky as wearing pajamas to school. (I even find myself disappointed when I pick a boring A.) So, I wash my father's car even though he insists the forecast is for rain. (It is and it does.) I eat a Marshmallow-Fluff-and-bologna sandwich for lunch. (That won't be a choice again anytime soon.) And I let my nail polish chip off instead of removing it. (This sounds like the tiniest, stupidest thing, but if you're a perfectionist, walking around with broken chips of purple on your nails is *worse* than eating a fluff-and-bologna sandwich.)

Let the games continue. . . .

Choice #5
What to Do on a Rainy, Boring Saturday

A) Call up Lynn and see if she wants to go to the library.

B) Call Christine (!) and see if she wants to make a soufflé—whatever that is.

C) Bury Billy and Tish's soccer uniforms in the cemetery.

D) Improvise something with my tools for Grandpa. No instructions, just instinct.

I play with the tiles, rearranging them around my desk. A with its little l underneath it, B_3, C_3, D_2. 1-3-3-2. 1-3-3-2. Even I have to admit that I'm stalling. But the thought of Christine answering the phone and laughing at my invitation—to make a soufflé, no less!—completely paralyzes me. Ten Mary Poppins with a million spoonfuls of sugar could not make *that* choice go down. I can almost hear the dial tone of Christine hanging up on me as I finally choose my tile. I'm relieved when it's a D until the word *improvise* settles like an anvil in my stomach. I'm sure I can rearrange the letters in *improvise* until I come up with something a little less scary. But all the rearranging in the world won't change the fact that I have to make something with no plans. I take the tools from my desk and shuffle down to the basement.

Like a surgeon before an operation, I line up the bits of wood and wire, first by length, then by type. I find a piece of driftwood, pale and washed by time and ocean, and run it through my fingers. My mind goes to the small saw I use to cut wood into the familiar rectangle shape.

Uh-uh-uh, the letter D scolds. You can't make the safe picture frame you always make with Grandpa. Im-pro-vise.

I stare at the driftwood and pretend. If I *were* creative, what would I do?

You *are* creative, I tell myself. Look at how you jumble all those letters around! You're an alphabet magician! Can you at least *pretend* to be confident for one minute of one day?

Yeah, right.

I put the driftwood down and take a few different lengths of wire. I stretch them out, then put them back on the workbench in frustration. Maybe if I watch TV, I'll get inspired. Inspirational television—now *there's* an oxymoron.

I pick up the wires again, twirling them nervously. I've been doing everything the letters have asked me to do— things much more difficult than this. I look down at the wires in my hand. I've twirled them into one thick strand, almost like the gnarled trunk of a small tree. I spread the ends of the four pieces of wire so they are facing different angles. When I flatten the ends, they look like roots. I place the tree on top of the small piece of driftwood and bend it slightly. If I add pieces of wire to the top and bend them in different directions, they might look like branches.

The next time I look at the clock, an hour and a half has gone by. The tree looks frail, as if hurricane winds are blowing and its roots are digging into the earth for dear life. It's raw and beautiful and I'm so proud, I want to burst. I run upstairs to show Mom.

"Great," she says. She folds the towels into uneven stacks, ready to topple. "Very rustic."

"Is that good?" I ask. The stacks of towels make me nervous. I refold a few and straighten the crooked piles.

"Very good." She nods. "You should call Grandpa."

Since the rain has stopped, I walk over to his apartment, carrying the tree inside a small cardboard box.

Grandpa's apartment is on the top floor of a large brick building on the way downtown. Since my grandma died, he lives by himself. Lynn calls Grandpa's place "the little church on Thurston Street" because of all the statues he has. Jesus, Mary, St. Joseph, St. Jude, St. Francis of Assisi all have their designated place on the bookshelves and tabletops. There are also dishes of candy on the television, but the candy is always stuck together and looks like it's been there for ages.

"Well, well." Grandpa turns the tree around in his hands. His smile twinkles. "Where'd you find the instructions for this?"

"Very funny." I frown, but inside, my heart is pounding.

"POROUS MAID," he says.

I smile at our game, then begin to jumble the letters around in my head. Maybe improvising has cleared some space in there, because today I don't need a piece of paper to come up with the answer.

"I AM SO PROUD?" I ask.

He nods with a grin.

"Thank you," I say, and I mean it. "It's a gift. I just want to borrow it to show Darcy."

He places the tree back in the box. "I guess I should have given you those tools earlier. I can't wait to see what else you come up with."

A lump begins to form in my throat. I never would have made this if it weren't for Multiple Choice, and I don't know if I'll have the courage to make anything else original again.

"Maybe next time, a whole forest," he says.

Suddenly his enthusiasm chokes me like a brightly colored scarf. I'm a fake. A real fake. It's an oxymoron I am too ashamed to share with Grandpa.

But for some reason, I don't feel like torturing myself today. I *did* make this and I *am* proud of it. In fact, I not only made this, I made up the whole Multiple Choice game. I am creative, I am imaginative. Multiple Choice is doing everything I wanted it to do. I'm changing, I'm growing. And I'm still Monica.

```
              2
              A
1 OPEN              4           6
              Y     5 SPONTANEOUS
              T        T         I
              H        A         M
              I        G         I
            3 NOTHING  N       7 DARING
              G        A
                       N
                       T
```

DOWN

2. _____ is possible.

4. My life is no longer _____.

6. The old Monica was _____.

ACROSS

1. My options are _____.

3. _____ can get in my way.

5. The new Monica is _____.

7. The new Monica is _____.

Darcy holds the tree I made up to the sun. "Look at how the light reflects off the wire on this side." She twirls the piece so I can see it. "Are you going to enter this in the craft fair?"

Justin runs by, wearing only a Batman cape and socks.

"I haven't really thought about it," I answer. Of course I *have* thought about it, about a million times, but I'm too frightened to think about it for long. And if I ask the letters if I should do it, I just might have to.

"It's important for people to see your work." Darcy puts the tree back in the box. "Your work is an expression of you."

It makes me uncomfortable when Darcy talks this way; I'm not really used to it. At my house, my parents are concerned with chores getting done and bills getting paid. We never really talk about ourselves and our dreams.

"I'm sure the fair is stupid," I say.

"People taking the time to *create* things is never stupid," Darcy answers. "Check it out."

"I will," I answer, but I probably won't. Although if she keeps asking me, I might have to.

Darcy fills a pitcher with water and takes a glass from

the cupboard. "I'm going downstairs. Time for me to get off my high horse and create something of my own." She smiles. "Why don't you and Justin walk down to Gray's for an ice cream?"

At the word *ice cream* Justin runs to the front door.

"Hey, Batman, better put some clothes on," Darcy calls over her shoulder. "You'll give away your secret identity."

Walking to the ice-cream shop, I wish I had brought Lynn. Justin likes her and the time always goes by faster when she's here. I stop by her house, but she's not home. I ask Tish if she wants to go instead.

Justin tries to take off his shirt while we wait in line, but I convince him to keep it on. I order black raspberry cones for the two of us and a maple walnut for Tish. She seems happy that I asked her to come; sometimes I'm so wrapped up in my own life that I forget she'd like to do something with me once in a while.

Tish and Justin race to the picnic table near the fence and I follow closely behind, hoping he doesn't drop his cone. He doesn't drop it running, but as he takes his first lick, the ball of black raspberry topples to the ground. I've been around enough of the day care kids to know what happens next.

Justin erupts, all right, but not into tears. Into laughter.

"Boom!" he says. "Like a water balloon. A purple water balloon." He is in stitches and Tish and I are speechless.

He picks up the melting ball and throws it—PLOP. More laughter.

"Boom!" Tish joins in. I follow them in amazement, finally interjecting a few "Booms!" of my own.

I figure we'll have to walk back to the house for more money—I don't have enough in my pocket—but he's not even thinking about a replacement. He's poking the ice cream with a stick, getting it to run in rivulets across the parking lot.

I try to figure out why I'm upset and he is unfazed.

It's unfair that he gets to be so easygoing, so free from bother, and I'm trapped and suffocated by all the rules governing my life. In my head, of course, but what difference does *that* make? I am envious of a four-year-old. Imagine trusting the world so much that you know there'll always be another ice-cream cone. That's just not the world I live in.

When we all get back to Darcy's house, Justin has forgotten about his ice cream and asks to see my kaleidoscope, which is in my backpack. I've never let him touch it before, and since I haven't played the Game yet today, I ask Tish to keep an eye on Justin as I head for the bathroom. I quickly make up a list with my normal choice, dumb choice, mean choice, and charitable choice. I reach in my velvet bag and feel for the four letters. When I choose the letter, I am shocked by my choice. I stare at the D tile, unsure of what to do next.

But I know what I have to do.

I return to the living room, remove the kaleidoscope from its box, and hand it to Justin. "You can have it," I say.

"Have it? For today?" he asks.

"For forever," I answer.

"What!" Tish says. "It's your favorite thing in the world!"

"I want you to have it," I tell Justin.

He runs circles around the room, holding it over his head. I follow him, arms extended, making sure he doesn't drop it.

He'd only asked to *see* it, for crying out loud. Why did I put down *giving* it to him as my sacrificial choice? And not only giving it to him, but NEVER LOOKING INSIDE IT AGAIN?

"I'm telling Mom," Tish adds. "That was a gift from Grandpa."

"It's mine. I can do whatever I want with it."

"You never even let me use it for more than a minute," she says.

I lie on the floor and show Justin how to turn the focus wheel. After about ten minutes, he tosses it on the couch, takes off his shirt, and asks if he can watch a Coyote-and-Road-Runner cartoon. I watch the show with him, but most of my attention is still on my kaleidoscope. *Justin will only break it, he doesn't love it as much as I do, it was a present from my grandfather. . . .* But I know these are silly excuses for me to break the Ground Rules. And breaking the rules is something I just can't do.

Choice #8
Billy and Tish Are Out—
I'm Stuck with My Parents

A) Finish my history report.

B) Give myself a haircut with the nail clippers.

C) Erase Dad's big presentation from his computer while he's at rehearsal.

D) Give Mom a pedicure.

I don't think I've ever touched my mother's feet before.

Oh, well—no thinking, just doing. I gather up bottles of nail polish and remover and a jar of cotton balls and head to the playroom.

Mom is wiping down the painting table and putting away wooden beads. She cleans like someone who has spent half her life doing it—one hand swipes the beads away, the other scrapes at the dried paint. I pick up the loose papers from the table and stack them neatly away.

"Peter had a meltdown today," she says. "Purple paint everywhere."

I try not to focus on the strip of purple she has missed along the edge of the table. "You've been working so hard," I say. "Why don't you just sit and rest for a while?"

"I've been waiting for a time to rest," she answers. "Since 1989."

I drag her reluctantly to the overstuffed chair. If I'm going to do it, I might as well do it right. I run to the bathroom and return with a wet facecloth. "Here, put this on your face."

"Monica, really, I don't have time."

I gently push her back in the chair and place the wet cloth over her eyes. She actually seems to relax a bit. I sort through the nail polish, eventually deciding on a deep wine.

She lifts up the cloth to find me taking off her slippers. "May I ask what you're doing?"

"I just thought a pedicure might relax you. Like one of those spas rich ladies go to," I respond.

"Those rich ladies don't have to thaw out chicken for tomorrow, do three loads of laundry, or mend two soccer uniforms."

"Just ten minutes." Maybe because my expression is so perky, she sighs and relents.

I begin by filing her nails, which look neglected and uneven. Excusing myself, I run to the bathroom closet and find an old pumice stone to smooth her heels.

"Boy, what did I do to deserve the queen's treatment?" she asks.

I tell her I just feel like doing it. And after a few minutes, that made-up excuse really is true. I rub lotion on her feet, then apply the polish, dabbing at the stray spots of red with a Q-tip. She sighs a few times and sinks deeper into the chair.

"You know what I miss?" my mother asks. "Bodysurfing."

It must be the fumes from the nail polish remover that are making my mother lose her mind.

"When I was your age, that was all I did. Dive into the waves, swim out over my head, and wait for a wave big enough to carry me to shore." She lifts up the facecloth and peeks a twinkling eye at me. "That feeling when the wave's barreling down on you and your timing has to be just right. You decide when to go, then let the wave take you, the water pounding your back, driving you onto shore. God, I loved those times."

"Why don't you go anymore?" I ask.

"It was too hard to go when you kids were little, then your father started traveling and I opened up the business." She covers her eyes and leans back in the chair.

"Maybe we should go this summer," I suggest. "It would be fun."

I'm not sure if she wants to have a discussion about beach activities or just rest, so I continue to work. I apply the last coat and admire my work—ten glistening little rubies. After a few minutes, my mother's breath deepens and I realize she is asleep. I cover her with the afghan, careful not to let the cotton touch the wet polish. Before I leave, I scrape the ribbon of purple paint from the table and pick out the random beads from the crayon bin. Then I gather my beautician's tools and leave the room quietly.

I know I don't have to, but I take out the chicken and put a load of towels in the wash.

I wonder if my mother is happy with her life. Is she living the life she dreamed of when she was my age? Will I?

I sit at the counter and peel a banana. The more I think, the more difficult the questions get. Will my life be what

I want it to be? How *do* I want it to be? But worrying about the future is too scary, so I concentrate on worrying about the present.

The good news is that I have been obsessing less since I invented Multiple Choice. Maybe it's because worrying about things like wearing a bridesmaid dress or ruining Dad's computer files are so insane that they send my mind into overload and it finally stops. Like too many switches being thrown in a fuse box, they cancel each other out. I don't know how long Multiple Choice will last, but for now, I'll stick with it. It's working.

I go back to check on Mom. She looks so comfortable that I decide not to wake her. Maybe she's dreaming about riding that just-right wave to shore. Maybe she and I aren't so different after all; we're just longing for different kinds of perfection.

```
U  C  M  X  Z  G  N  I  T  I  C  X  E  E
L  N  N  P  L  P  X  M  B  E  H  A  S  D
M  P  E  O  E  U  Y  O  P  H  T  G  U  M
S  R  W  E  S  P  O  I  T  N  L  D  W  X
D  P  Q  A  Z  K  E  Y  B  V  N  M  U  Y
R  T  Y  P  O  R  R  E  I  Z  S  E  R  T
R  U  E  O  F  H  V  N  Y  R  A  C  S  I
M  V  N  E  R  S  P  W  S  X  P  O  K  L
E  S  T  R  A  N  G  E  C  V  Q  A  I  K
P  O  I  U  Y  T  R  E  W  Q  A  S  D  F
```

Mrs. Coleman had to take Peter's brother to the emergency room, so Peter is here with us for dinner, sucking his spaghetti into his mouth as loud as humanly possible. My mother certainly doesn't treat him like company either because she starts right in with the words I've been expecting to hear for the past nine days.

"Monica, are you okay? You've been acting a little strange lately."

I twirl my spaghetti around my fork. "Everything's fine," I answer.

"She tried to lead everybody on the bus in a *song* today," Tish says, still in shock from this afternoon's choice. "She stood in the aisle and sang 'Ninety-nine Bottles of Beer' like we were all going on some camping trip together. Everybody thought she was insane." She glares at me and says for the fiftieth time, "I have never been so embarrassed in my life."

Hey, do you think that was *easy*? I want to say. Do you know how much courage it took to get up in the middle of forty people and start singing that stupid song? I'm a warrior, an artist. You should appreciate me. (Just be glad I didn't pick B—"Puff the Magic Dragon.")

"I want to know what's going on," my mother continues. "Are you putting yourself under too much pressure with finals?"

"No, of course not."

Peter stares back and forth at the two of us like we're playing Ping-Pong.

Mom raises her voice a notch. "Don't say 'no, of course not' like you've never done that before. You were physically ill for two weeks last June, remember?"

Of course I remember; I was the one puking every day. She makes it sound like I *enjoyed* it. How could she possibly know how difficult it is to ace a test for Ms. O'Connell?

"I ran into Mr. Bergeron at Billy's game today. He told me you wore pajamas to school last week."

"I have pajamas," Peter says. "Rugrats with Tommy and Chuckie."

I cough out a chunk of pasta, then try to come up with the best excuse to give my mother. *Lynn and I were practicing for a play? It was a dare? Everything else was in the wash?*

"I lost a bet," I finally tell her.

"Well, here's one thing you *can* bet on," my mother says. "Any more of this foolishness and we're making an appointment with your guidance counselor."

Great, Ms. Mitchell. Always late, always nervous, always covering her mustache with her hand—a real help.

My mother's face softens. "I appreciated the pedicure. But I want to make sure you're not too stressed."

"I don't know what's going on, but I'll tell you one thing," Tish says. "I'm walking back and forth to school for the rest of the year. I'm not going to be seen with Monica until she starts acting normal."

Whatever that is.

Ah, Tish. If you only knew. I had thought of telling her about Multiple Choice last week, but when I asked the tiles, they told me no. And looking at her now, so worried about her popularity and easy existence, I'm glad I didn't.

"Well, Monica," my mother finishes. "If you need to talk, I'm here for you."

"I'm fine, I'm fine, I'm fine." I bring my plate to the counter as if to emphasize the point. Thanks a lot, Mr. Bergeron. Nice going.

But I still feel bad about Tish, so after dinner, I approach her at the sink. "I'm sorry you were embarrassed," I say. "I just felt like a little sing-along, that's all." I grab a dish towel and dry the pan she has just finished. "Want to watch TV?"

She shakes her head. "Go away."

On another day, she might have sung along with me, or at least thought it was funny. But today Bobby Atamian was on the bus, and she's been obsessing about him for months. (Not *really* obsessing, just junior obsessing; I'd have a lot to teach her if she *really* wanted to obsess.) When she approached him after we got off, he looked at her, then at me, and kept walking. The guy definitely could not take a joke.

I spend the rest of the night trying to get Tish to like me again, with no luck. I join the Chutes and Ladders game she's playing with Peter, but as soon as I sit down she leaves. I even offer her half of my Kit Kat and she turns *it* down.

By the time I go to bed, I'm mad at Tish, sick of trying to make her happy. I take the T, I, S, and H tiles out of the Scrabble box and shuffle them around my desk. Her name's got a few easy anagrams, one of them a swearword I never say. But tonight it sums up my feelings to a T. (No pun intended.)

I don't think I'm imagining this, but of course I might be. It seems that people are beginning to think about me differently. Kids at school seem to be more curious, less ready to pigeonhole me into a certain kind of behavior. Even Nice Shirt Christine laughed when I howled like a wolf in the middle of Ms. Cotter's media lab spiel. It's not that I want to be Christine's friend, God forbid, but I also don't like being treated as if I think I'm so perfect. Which I'm not, of course—that's my biggest problem.

Mike the Mosquito even asks me to come to the party he's having Saturday night. Lynn is visiting her grand-mother this weekend, so I'd have to go it alone. I shake the letters inside my locker and ask whether I should. Vowel—yes. Consonant—no. It's a three-out-of-four chance of not going, which suits me fine. As fate would have it, though, I pick the A.

Better start thinking of some good party options.

Choice #10
The Mosquito's Party

A) See if the new girl, Nicole, wants to go to the party with me.

B) Mention the phrase *cookie dough* in five conversations during the party.

C) Follow Joey DeSalvo around all night and tell all his friends I'm his new girlfriend. (This choice is not mean to Joey; it's mean to *me*.)

D) Walk around the party with an empty coffee can, taking donations for the retired teachers' fund. (A real antipopularity stunt if there ever was one.)

B.

I suppose making conversation about cookie dough is better than the entire eighth grade thinking I have a crush on Joey. Even *I* admit that choice was going way too far.

I try not to bug the Mosquito by asking too many questions the day before—*Are your parents going to be home? How many people will be there? What time should my mother pick me up?* In fact, these questions worry me more than they do my mother. She drops me off at seven and tells me to have a good time.

Mrs. Greendale, the Mosquito's mother, takes my coat at the door and shows me to the family room. The furniture and knickknacks are all antiques—certainly not the kind of house I would have pictured Mike the Mosquito living in. When he buzzes down the hall at school, he leaves several people knocked over in his wake.

Downstairs, the CD blares and Janelle and Bruce play guitars. Christine sits on the couch with Karen, and she nudges her when I walk in. Mike comes over and says hello, then walks me over to the food and soda. Here goes.

I look at the creamy dip in the middle of the plate of vegetables. "Nice dip." I pause, feeling ridiculous. "Looks like cookie dough."

Mike stares at the dip and shakes his head. "Whatever." He points to the cans of soda and leaves to talk to Joey.

This is not a good idea, this is not a good idea, I tell myself over and over. What was I thinking? I feel my body crumble when Christine and Karen approach.

"How come you're not wearing pajamas?" Karen asks.

I can't tell if she's trying to pick a fight or make conversation.

Christine doesn't even wait till I can answer. "Oh, is this a sleep over?" she asks. "I'm sure Mrs. Mosquito will be pleased to hear about that." We all laugh, and for a minute I think this could be a regular conversation. But then I remember that I have to insert *cookie dough* into the conversation and my stomach churns all over again.

"I went to a sleep over last night. We were up all night, eating cookie dough ice cream." It's stretching the truth—I slept over at Lynn's house last week, and the only things we ate were popcorn and chocolate-covered raisins. But now I'm two *cookie doughs* down, three to go.

"So," Christine says. "Are you acing Mr. Bergeron's class?"

"She's acing every class," Karen says.

"You are too," I tell Christine.

Christine smiles smugly.

Karen leans in close. "In sports, she holds the record at

her last school for the most soccer goals in a season. Girls and boys."

I imagine Christine running across the soccer field, all cheetah, no fear. "That's great."

"Yeah, well, it was no big deal." She wanders over to the soda, with Karen following behind.

See? A totally normal conversation, just what you wanted. You're doing it, you're changing, I think to myself.

But I know Christine will be punching into her job Monday morning, that this was just a brief respite from her teasing. Besides, I have to use three more *cookie doughs* within the next hour. I approach Joey DeSalvo, who I figure won't be paying attention. It'll be like mentioning cookie dough to a hammer.

"Hi."

He looks at me blankly, staring at the television with the sound turned off. Two men are kick boxing in an airplane hangar. I stand next to his chair and watch too.

"God, all that fighting must make you hungry. Probably need a snack afterward. Some cookie dough ice cream or something." I wince at my own words.

He doesn't even blink as he stares at the screen. For a minute, I think about reciting some nursery rhymes or product jingles to make sure he's still among the living, but Janelle has turned down the radio and is playing her guitar for the group. I like Janelle; we were in the chess club together two years ago. She's the best musician in our school, and when she begins to sing, three or four others join in.

After Joey leaves, I settle into his chair, wondering what it could possibly feel like to be sure enough of yourself to sit in the middle of a party, play guitar, and sing. Although I suppose it's not any more difficult than singing "Ninety-nine Bottles of Beer" on the bus.

Janelle sings a few traditional songs and then starts making up songs about things in the room—the kick-boxing movie, Mike's mother's antiques. People shout out topics and she makes up a few lines of a song right on the spot. No Multiple Choice or anything.

"Any other ideas?" she asks after singing about Miss Cotter. "What should we sing about?"

Dare I say it?

"Cookie dough ice cream." I try to gauge my voice to see if it sounds convincing.

Janelle laughs and makes up a verse about fighting for the last spoonful of ice cream with her sister. When she's done, everyone applauds.

And for a few minutes, I feel like everything really *is* perfect. Most everyone is singing now—except Joey, Mike, and Dan, who are playing darts in the next room. I sing along softly, still unsure about being here with this new group of people.

I don't even notice Christine sidling up beside me. "Monica Devon. No damn voice." She shakes her head as if I'm throwing off everyone in the room. There's no way she could know how cautious I am about singing in front of other people. When your mother tells your sister a thousand times what a great voice she has and never says anything about yours, you begin to get the hint. I immediately stop singing but continue to tap my hand on the arm of the couch, keeping time, acting as if I didn't hear her. *THIS does not count. This DOES not count. This does NOT count. This does not COUNT.* Janelle takes a break after the next song, when Mr. Greendale brings down several boxes of pizza.

I have fifteen minutes before my mother comes. I opt for an easy way to end the game. I take a slice of mushroom pizza and walk over to Janelle.

"You're good at making up songs," I say. "That one about cookie dough was great."

Done, finally, over.

"It's not so hard to do. I've been making up songs since I was little."

We talk for a few minutes until Joey and Mike get into a fight about what movie to watch. I thank God one thousand times that I didn't have to pretend to be Joey's girlfriend. A fate worse than any kind of ice-cream flavor.

When my mother picks me up, she's exceptionally happy, that forced kind of enthusiasm she uses when she's worried that I won't fit in and will stress myself into a frenzy. "Everything all right?" she asks.

I bury my face in my hands. "No one talked to me, everyone made fun of me, they were making up songs about me."

"Monica!"

I sit up in my seat with a smile. "I'm just kidding. It was fine."

First she looks mad, then she smiles too. "I'm glad you had fun."

And when I think about it, I *did* have fun, even though I spent half the night inserting weird phrases into my conversations. I should have made up Multiple Choice years ago.

"Let's pick up some ice cream to bring home for everyone," my mother suggests.

"How about cookie dough?" And I laugh at my own joke for a good five minutes.

Choice #12
Doing Errands with Dad, I Act Like . . .

A) Normal Monica—whoever that is.

B) A girl raised in the wild.

C) Rizzo in *Grease*. (This choice will be really nasty if I have to smoke and swear in front of Dad.)

D) Florence Nightingale.

I close my eyes and choose.

Yet another B.

I'm almost happy for this choice, as if acting like the real Monica all day would be too much work.

Dad claps and tells us to hurry before I have a chance to prepare. Oh, well, have to wing it. Something I've almost gotten good at lately.

We park the car on Boylston Street and I jump out before Dad shuts off the engine.

"Hold on there, Monica," he says.

Because I'm swinging from the No Parking During Snow Emergency sign, I barely hear him. Billy laughs when he sees me, then jumps up and tries to hit the top of the sign. Tish grabs on too and soon the three of us are a pile of giggling fools on the sidewalk.

" 'Tis the big city that excites you so?" Dad asks. He forges on, toward the Common.

The remains of a Snickers bar on the sidewalk catch my eye. I hold it up for Billy and Tish to see. "We better keep this for later," I grunt.

Billy swoops down on an almost empty bottle of Evian.

"We'll need all the provisions we can get." Soon the three of us are filling Billy's backpack with stuff we find on the street: a broken comb, an empty Tic Tac box, a baby's mitten. Tish and I explode in laughter when Billy picks up a tube of Chap Stick, removes the cover, and spreads the salve across his lips. My father, not knowing what Tish and I are shrieking about, turns around briefly, shaking his head.

"Might one venture to guess that a voyage to yonder provision house would bring such simple pleasure?" he says.

Billy wipes his mouth with his sleeve and the three of us run to catch up to my father. He senses we're in the mood for fun and doesn't let us down.

Dad stands with his legs apart like a cowboy during a shoot-out. "Well, partners, what do we have here?" he asks, pointing up ahead to a meter maid slipping a ticket onto the windshield of a blue convertible.

We all cringe in horror. "We've got to do something!" I shout this as if I'm wearing torn shorts, swinging from a tree.

My father puts his hand in his pocket and comes up with a handful of change. "Quick! Before the constable sees us!" He hands us each a quarter and we stare at him, not knowing what to do next. But it only takes a minute for us to follow his lead. Soon the four of us are racing down Boylston Street, filling every empty meter, only seconds away from the meter cop, whose pen is poised to write another ticket. We go through all our change, and when the meter maid catches up to us, Billy asks strangers walking by for a quarter to feed the meter. The fourth person—a woman in a red cape—hands us two and we feed the rest of the meters up to Arlington Street. The meter maid tips her hat when she passes us, probably glad for the break in routine.

If my mother were here, she'd scold my father for wasting money. But Dad invests money in a different way than Mom. "Think of all those people we saved from getting tickets," he says, finally using his normal voice. "You little Robin Hoods deserve a reward." We tumble into the diner, still flushed with the excitement of beating the system.

As we squeeze into the booth, giggling and happy, I realize it is the most fun I have ever had with Billy and Tish. Sure, Billy teases me all the time, but he can be adventurous. And Tish, unlike me, is flexible, always eager to try new things. That thought leads to another one, which I try to ignore but can't. *They like you better this way. They don't like you when you're Monica. They like you better when you're someone else.* I gather up all my wild-child-ness and laugh and joke with my family while the waitress brings our hamburgers.

I try to shake off this feeling but it stays, settling in for a long visit. *Multiple Choice is changing you on the outside, but nothing's changing on the inside. You're still obsessing. Now you're not obsessed with everything, just one thing—Multiple Choice. You haven't gotten better—you've gotten worse. You might as well quit Multiple Choice tomorrow.*

But I won't. I'm stuck on some kind of roller-coaster ride that I can't just jump out of. I feel like I'm headed for a collision.

I ignore the sports announcer voice as best I can, still being the best wild child I can be. I empty out the napkin dispenser one by one, dealing the rectangle napkins to my father, Billy, and Tish like cards. But it's a forced spontaneity—another torturous oxymoron.

"Hey, Mon," Billy says. "Catch." He throws his pickle across the table.

I eat it savagely, like a hungry girl trapped on a desert island. Which I guess is kind of what I am.

Choice #13
Looking For a Way to Hate Myself Even More

A) I will never play Multiple Choice again.

B) I will smoke in the girls' room between every class until a teacher catches me.

C) I will write something nasty about Lynn at school.

D) I will take Tish's new Doc Martens—the ones she saved up for—and bring them to the Goodwill drop-off center.

No, no, no. I look at the letter again, angry at my decision to make the choices harder and scare myself away from Multiple Choice. I have finally gone too far.

C.

Why did I give myself such ridiculous options—I *love* Lynn. Well, that's the end of Multiple Choice. Acting like a wild child is one thing; hurting Lynn is another. Over. Period. Done.

Good. This is a good thing. A safe way to get off the Multiple Choice roller coaster.

I empty the A, B, C, and D tiles into the Scrabble box and put my velvet bag away.

Had to quit sometime anyway.

During school, I try to keep my mind on my classes, but whenever I open my backpack, I can almost feel the void left by the missing letters. Several times during the day, I reach for the velvet bag, wanting to hear the tiles clacking inside. I spend the morning feeling like some zombie in drug rehab. Drop it. Let it go.

In the bathroom mirror between classes, I cheer myself

on. You can do it. You don't need Multiple Choice to break free of rules. *You're* in charge, not the letters. But my heart beats faster and faster. I'm in the bathroom at the end of the old west wing, near the science labs. Deep down, I know why I came here today. If I write something bad about Lynn up here, hardly anyone will see it, least of all her. And then technically I can still keep playing.

I lock myself in the stall, take out a pen, and start to write. But the tiles are too smooth and the ink doesn't hold. Maybe if I write it and it's invisible, it will still count.

I find a black marker in my bag and start to write again. It's a permanent marker, no changing my mind. I use the smallest-possible letters the tip will allow. During Ms. Hodgett's class I wrote down some things about Lynn that would be considered bad but not *that* bad. I told myself I wasn't going to actually do it, I just wanted to see what I could come up with. Maybe a part of me knew I would be writing those words for real.

LYNN KELLY GIVES DUMB BLONDES A BAD NAME

As soon as I read the words, I run my fingers across the tile to smudge them. But they don't move; I guess that's why they call it permanent ink. I don't use the toilet, but still flush so I won't seem suspicious. When I emerge from the stall, Tanya MacNie blasts into the room, pocketbook, hair, and Walkman flying.

"Mr. Donnelly's such a zabbo." She throws her stuff on the sink. "Do you have him?"

I sneak the marker into my bag and tell her I don't have Mr. Donnelly. My curiosity about words gets the better of me. "What's a zabbo?"

She looks at me like I have purple hair (which she does). "It's just a word," she answers. She hauls her stuff into the stall I just used. I don't want to be here when she's done, so I sneak out and head downstairs for English.

I take my seat next to Lynn without looking at her.

"Want some gum?" she asks.

I feel that if I take the stick she's holding, I'll be the biggest traitor in the world—as if I don't feel that way already.

"No thanks."

She tosses it on my desk. "Save it for later, then."

I unearth a smile from some phony place inside me. "Your highlights look great."

She seems puzzled. "They're a week old."

"I know; they just look good, that's all. You look really pretty."

She rolls her eyes but smiles. After class I tell her I have to talk to Ms. Hodgett about extra credit, so I won't be on the bus. I walk home, chewing the gum loudly, then I do something I never do. I swallow it. Let the hard lump of sugar—or whatever it is—grow into some kind of peppermint tumor.

I deserve it.

GIRL
BOARD

(Girl overboard . . .)

Mr. Bergeron pulls me aside after class. He's wearing a tie with bows and arrows and archery targets.

"I just want to make sure you're okay," he says.

"Is there a problem with my work?" I ask.

He fiddles with his glasses. "Your behavior just seems to be a little—I don't know—erratic lately." He looks at me with an expression of such care that it makes me want to cry.

"Things are fine," I say. "Really dandy." It's a word I've never used in my life.

"When I saw your mother last week, I mentioned my concern. I hope you don't mind."

"No, she told me." I try to detour the conversation. "I'm just finishing everything up before school ends."

He sits down on the corner of his desk. "Don't mind me. I'm a worrier. I always think the worst. I'm glad everything's okay."

"You worry about things too?"

"Oh, sure, all the time. Drives my wife crazy. She never worries about a thing."

"She's lucky," I say. I imagine his wife—some middle-aged woman with glasses and high heels dropping an ice-cream cone like Justin, and the two of them laughing hysterically.

"Sometimes it seems like there are so many choices. It's hard choosing the right one," he says.

"Sometimes it's not so hard," I say. (Maybe Mr. Bergeron would be a good candidate for Multiple Choice.)

"You've got such a great future ahead of you. I just want to make sure you live up to your full potential."

He *is* a worrier, maybe almost as good (or bad) as I am. I try to relieve his fears. "I *am* thinking about my future," I say. "In fact, I was talking to Miss Cotter today about entering the craft fair."

"Great, I'm glad to hear it."

Oh, boy. Now I have to find Miss Cotter before the end of the day in case he asks her about it. I leave the room almost skipping so he'll stop worrying.

After all, I know what that's like. I wouldn't wish it on anyone.

I'm walking home by myself when I hear Lynn hurrying up behind me. She's yelling for me to wait. There could be a hundred reasons why she wants me, but I still feel my spine stiffen. She's finally close enough that I can't pretend not to hear her anymore. When I see her angry, red face, I know what she wants.

"Did you or did you not write something bad about me in the bathroom?"

"What are you talking about?" I try to keep walking, but she stops me dead.

"Someone wrote that I give dumb blondes a bad name. Was it you?"

"How can you ask me that? I'm your best friend!" Turn the accusation around, make the other person feel guilty. The day care parents always do this to my mother when they're late.

"I thought you were my best friend until someone told me you were the one who wrote it. And you're not denying it." Her arms are crossed in front of her, and she's almost shaking.

"Of course I didn't do it! What's wrong with you?"

She calms down a bit. "I didn't think you did. I thought the whole story sounded made up."

A wave of relief washes over me. "I mean, really, Lynn. Come on."

She begins walking toward our street. "I know. It was stupid. I never should have listened to Tanya. She's a head case half the time. But who would write such a thing?"

"Someone sick, someone with no life." I realize when I answer that it's a pretty accurate description of me. "Try to forget about it."

"I suppose so." We walk in silence for a few blocks until she stops, triumphant.

"I was right about Mr. Bergeron and Miss Cotter. They were making plans to go to the Vineyard today. I heard them."

"I did too. They're going together for the weekend. With their families. Sorry to burst your bubble."

She doesn't even try to hide her disappointment. "I thought for sure they were together."

I tell Lynn about my conversation with Miss Cotter about the craft fair. And as we walk, it's like it always is with Lynn—easy, fun, familiar. Following the rules *does* make sense. I'm safe. Multiple Choice protects those who play.

When we get to our street, she takes my arm. "I'm sorry I accused you of writing that."

"Not a problem," I answer.

"I feel like you now, obsessing over this."

I shove her playfully.

"Why would Tanya lie to me about seeing you coming out of the stall with a marker? Why would she want us to fight?"

"Who knows," I say. "I'm never even up there."

Lynn starts to walk across the street to her house, then stops. "Up where?"

"Um, the second-floor bathroom."

She walks back toward me.

"I never said it was that bathroom."

I suddenly feel as if the temperature has dropped from sixty-eight to twenty-two degrees.

"Yes, you did. You said the second-floor bathroom."

"No, I didn't."

"Maybe I thought you did because Tanya takes all those science classes and that would be the bathroom she uses."

"That's the reason she said it was you," Lynn says. "Because she used it *before* biology and the writing wasn't there, then she used it *after* biology and it *was* there."

I head toward my house, trying to be nonchalant. "So then anybody who used the bathroom that period could have written it."

"NOBODY uses those bathrooms," Lynn screams. "You said so yourself." Her face is back to crimson. "Did you go up there?"

"No! I told you I didn't!"

"So if you and I go to Tanya's locker tomorrow and ask her if she saw you up there, she would say no?"

"Yes, I mean, no. Just because I may have gone up there doesn't mean I *wrote* anything." I tell myself to stay logical, stay calm.

"Oh, so now you were up there!"

My present sense of danger grows when I realize my mother could be in the house, ready to come out and see what's going on. "I was there, okay? But I didn't write anything. Jeez, is there a law against using the second-floor bathroom?"

Lynn surprises me by grabbing my pack from my shoulders. "What are you doing? Give that back!" I shout.

She dumps my pack onto the steps and rummages through the books, Kleenex, and paper until she finds what she's looking for.

She holds the black marker up to my face. "Is this what you used?"

The words are trapped inside me. I feel numb.

"Well?"

I still don't answer. *THIS does not count. This DOES not count . . .*

"TALK!" Lynn looks so mad, I barely recognize her.

I crouch on the steps, surrounded by my stuff. "Stop it, okay? It was me. I'm sorry."

Her voice quiets down and when I look up, I see she is crying. "How could you say that about me? We both know you're smarter than me—or I, whatever it is. But you never *once* made me feel stupid before."

"Of course you're not stupid." I begin to cry too.

"Then why did you do it?"

Even if I tell her about Multiple Choice—which I can't—she'd never understand. I pick up my books and put them back in my bag. "There is no why. Nothing that makes sense anyway. That's the crazy thing about it."

"Crazy? *You're* the one who's crazy. Wearing pajamas to school, singing on the bus. I was worried about you before; now I think you're sick." She's crying hard, snapping the scrunchie on her wrist over and over. "Why? I just want to know why."

But I can't tell her.

"Mon, come on. *Say* something."

But I don't.

After a few minutes, she runs into her house, still crying.

Because of the Game.

Because of me.

That was a giant, terrible mistake.

A huge, mammoth megamistake.

I wipe my eyes and go inside. From the kitchen window I watch Mom playing Ring-Around-the-Rosy with Peter, Charlie, and Melissa. Three years old—the same age Lynn and I were when she moved in across the street.

I start crying all over again.

Ashes, ashes, we all fall down.

A
AS
ASH
RASH
CRASH

When I call, Lynn's mother tells me she isn't home, even though I know she is. Lynn ignores me at school, and when I pass her a note in Mr. Bergeron's class, she rips it up without reading it.

I spend the class thinking about the time in fifth grade when we did a science project together. We made lava out of paraffin and orange food coloring and a volcano out of plaster. Lynn typed the report and I did the poster board. But even with all my stencils, markers, and rulers, I couldn't get that stupid three-part board the way I wanted it. I stenciled and erased, stenciled and erased one too many times until the cardboard finally ripped. My father drove me to the store to get another one, but they were closed. When I called Lynn up in tears, she came across the street in her pajamas and covered the torn board with fabric. She cut out felt letters and glued them on. Off the top of her head—without worrying. And even though the baking soda explosion made a mess of the table, we won first prize. She never once yelled at me for making her work twice as hard.

After math, I go into the girls' room next to our lockers

to see if I can find her. Claudia and Beth both look at me and giggle on their way out. It makes me wonder if Lynn has told anyone else about our fight. I head for my usual stall, but when I go to hang my pack on the hook, giant black letters stare back at me.

Mentally
Oppressed
Needy
Isolated
Crybaby
Attention starved

Dying to be right
Eager to please
Void of emotions
Obsessive
Nutjob

I run to the sink, wet a handful of paper towels, and try to rub it off. Damn permanent ink. I used small letters in an obscure bathroom; these are giant letters in the most used bathroom of the school. (And of course Lynn knows which stall I always use.)

When I see her in the hall later, I sneak up behind her. "Nice, really nice."

"I have no idea what you're talking about."

"I told you I was sorry, didn't I?"

Christine looks up from the water fountain just in time to see us walk by.

"Hey, Monica, you like word games. Check out the new one in the bathroom."

Lynn laughs, then turns to me. "It couldn't have been me—too many big words. I'm not that smart."

Christine approaches and asks Lynn if she wants to help decorate for the end-of-the-year party. Lynn looks back over her shoulder at me.

"Sure, I'd love to."

My mind races ahead—*Lynn and Christine will become best friends, their bond strengthened by how much they both hate me. They will tell each other Monica stories on the phone every night, twirling the curly cords around themselves, laughing, transforming every stupid thing I ever did or said into teenage legend. They'll have little code words and jokes and games that will revolve around me and how pathetic and laughable I am. When Mr. Bergeron or Miss Cotter says something in class that reminds Lynn and Christine of me, they will look at each other knowingly and nod, then talk about it the whole way home from school. . . .* I don't even try to stop myself from imagining the worst. After all, I was the one who started this whole thing.

I wipe my tears with the back of my hand. I deserve all of it for what I did to Lynn. She was my best friend and I hurt her and I'm eternally sorry.

I eat lunch by myself, a cafeteria martyr who is getting her just deserts.

TROUBI'MLE

(I'm in trouble . . .)

I've been playing again for more than two weeks; any normal person would have quit this stupid game by now. Therefore, one of these two statements must be true: Either I am not a normal person or there is no such thing as a normal person; therefore I cannot be one. I toss these questions over in my mind like philosophical pancakes. *Who is the real Monica? What am I doing?* These kinds of questions used to drive Lynn out of her mind. Too bad she's not around to hear them anymore.

Needless to say, I am not paying much attention to Justin, who has just finished disassembling an old telephone during an episode of *Arthur.* I suppose we're both doing the same thing this afternoon—looking inside things, trying to figure out what makes them work. At least he's getting some hand-eye coordination at the same time.

After *Arthur,* I take out the peanut butter and cut up an apple to make Justin's favorite snack. Darcy is downstairs painting; when I told her I decided to enter the craft fair, she grabbed my arms and swung me around the room like we were square dancing. I acted embarrassed but was pretty excited by her enthusiasm.

I don't feel like playing with puzzles, reading stories, or pretending to be a fire-breathing dragon. My insides feel like a guitar tuned too tightly, ready, almost hoping to snap. The tiles beckon me from inside my pack. A, B, C, D. A, B, C, D. For some inexplicable reason, losing my best friend is not enough.

I want to keep playing.

While Justin finishes eating, I lay out my choices.

Choice #16
Baby-sitting Justin

A) Play together outside on the swings.

B) Play his Barney tape (which Darcy hates) over and over until our brains are mush.

C) Lock Justin in his room.

D) Walk to the church up the street, light a candle, and let Justin run around naked.

Well, I didn't specify how long I'd have to lock Justin in his room—I'm getting sloppy in my play—so I quickly choose five minutes. With Darcy downstairs, it'll be hard to do it any longer.

I lead Justin to the sink to wash the peanut butter off his hands. "I've got an idea," I say. "Let's play prison. You be the prisoner and I'll be the guard."

We run upstairs to his room.

"I'll lock you in your cell and stand guard outside so you can't get out." I figure he'll play for a minute or so before getting distracted by the table of crayons and markers in his room. I close the door and lean against it. "You can't escape. Don't even try," I say in a gruff voice.

"But I didn't do anything!" He sounds so upset, I open the door to see if he's all right. He's smiling, fully into his role.

"I don't want to hear a peep out of you." I close the door and start timing the five minutes again.

I hear him drag a chair across the room. He bangs on the door. "Let me out! Let me out!"

When I look at my watch, only a minute and a half has

gone by. Like sitting through a class with Ms. Emerson, five minutes can be an eternity. I keep my eye on the basement door to make sure Darcy's not coming upstairs. I hear more dragging and scraping inside the room and hope the five minutes is up soon. It's the longest I've ever had Justin out of my sight. I figure he has given up the game in favor of coloring. Fifteen seconds to go.

But the next few seconds unfold like a slow-motion scene in an action movie when the hero runs away from a building before it explodes. The first thing I hear is the sound of scraping metal, followed by a sharp wail. My instinct is to burst through the door and make sure he's all right.

Here's the pathetic part.

The really sick part.

The first thing I do is look at my watch to see if the five minutes are up.

Eight seconds to go.

They are the longest eight seconds of my life. I know it's wrong, I really do, but I follow the rules and wait for the eight seconds to pass. As much as I have hated myself on and off during the last fourteen years, none of that self-hatred comes close to how much I detest myself during these few moments. While the second hand inches toward the twelve, I know that something inside me has snapped off and broken.

When I finally run into the room, Justin is nowhere to be found. The window near his bed is missing its screen. I stick my head out the open space and see Justin and the screen lying in the bushes one floor below. He's not moving.

I race down the stairs two at a time. When I reach him, he's holding one of his eyes, screaming. I try to lift him from the bush, but he's too hysterical. I run back inside to get Darcy.

When she sees my face, she yanks off her Walkman and races upstairs with me. She lifts Justin from the bushes and tries to examine his eye. But he's screaming so much, she can't.

"Come with me." She opens the door to the backseat of her car and hurries me inside. She places Justin in my arms and jumps behind the wheel.

Sometimes it takes something drastic to realize how wrong your life is, how desperately you need to change. Right now I want to go back to Justin's room and jump out the window myself over and over again. Fast-forward, rewind, fast-forward, rewind. Until my mind just stops. I hold Justin close and his sobbing softens.

"I'm so sorry," I whisper.

"I was trying to escape. I didn't want to be a prisoner," he says.

I hug him close. My sentiments exactly.

THIS does not count. This DOES not count. This does NOT count. This does not COUNT. THIS does not count. This DOES not count. This does NOT count. This does not COUNT. THIS does not count. This DOES not count. This does NOT count. This does not COUNT. THIS does not count. This DOES not count. This does NOT count. This does not COUNT. THIS does not count. This DOES not count. This does NOT count. This does not COUNT. THIS does not count. This DOES not count. This does NOT count. This does not COUNT. THIS does not count. This DOES not count. This does NOT count. This does not COUNT. THIS does not count. This DOES not count. This does NOT count. This does not COUNT. THIS does not count. This DOES not count. This does NOT count. This does not COUNT. THIS does not count. This DOES not count. This does NOT count. This does not COUNT. THIS does not count. This DOES not count. This does NOT count. This does not COUNT. THIS does not count. This DOES not count. This does NOT count. This does not COUNT. THIS does not count. This DOES not count. This does NOT count. This does not COUNT. THIS does not count. This DOES not count. This does NOT count. This does not COUNT. THIS does not count. This DOES not count. This does NOT count. This does not COUNT. THIS does not count. This DOES not count. This does NOT count. This does not COUNT. THIS does not count. This DOES not count. This does NOT count. This does not

Count us among the lucky ones; we only had to wait twenty minutes in the emergency room. Nevertheless, they are the worst twenty minutes of my life. (Not counting the eight seconds outside Justin's room.) I apologize profusely, making up an excuse about leaving Justin to go to the bathroom and the door to his room jamming. I might be imagining things, but it seems as if Darcy's attitude toward me grows colder by the minute. The receptionist finally calls Justin's name and I wait another forty-five terrible minutes while Darcy and Justin meet with the doctors.

Darcy emerges after a long time, holding Justin. "His cornea is scratched. We'll have to wait and see if he needs surgery."

I burst into tears. "This is all my fault."

She doesn't disagree. "He'll wear an eye patch for three weeks," she says. "It might heal on its own." Darcy pushes open the door to the parking lot. "Let's get out of here."

Once we get on the highway, she turns toward me. "Are you going to tell me what really happened?"

It's the "really" that gets to me, as if she didn't buy my excuse about leaving Justin to go to the bathroom. My silence only fuels Darcy's temper.

When we pull into her driveway, she yanks the emergency brake so hard, I'm afraid it's going to bust through the roof. She carries Justin into the house while I follow a few steps behind with the bag of instructions and ointments from the hospital. She settles him into bed with a stack of books.

All I want to do is run home, jump into my closet, shut the door, and die. My hand rests on the latch to the screen door. "Darcy, I'm so sorry. If there's anything I can do . . ."

"Where are you going? We're not done here."

Please let me leave.

"You've never been a good liar, Monica. I want to know what happened. Sit down."

I choose the kitchen stool with the torn vinyl. I usually can't bear to feel the rip against my skin, but it seems fitting now. Darcy's right about lying—look what happened with Lynn.

I feel the tears inch their way down my cheeks. "It's been a really bad few days. I am so, so sorry. For everything."

She pours us glasses of lemonade and waits. Probably some guidance counselor technique to get guilty kids like me to talk.

"It's kind of hard to explain," I say.

"Try me."

"It's this game I made up, see? It was supposed to make my life better."

"And you were playing that game with Justin? What was it, some kind of truth-or-dare thing?"

"Not really."

She waits again. What am I supposed to say?

She continues to wait, then pounds her fist on the counter. "Goddamn it, Monica! What happened?"

Her fist hitting the Formica sounds like a stick of dynamite going off, exploding the dam inside my brain. I don't even have to think; the words tumble out with the tears. Not just about playing prisoner and Justin falling through the screen, but about Multiple Choice, the Ground Rules, the cookie dough, Lynn. . . . The words sound scrambled and mixed up and I wait for Darcy to yell at me and tell me to slow down. She doesn't.

After the words run out, I sit quietly and cry.

Several minutes later Darcy finally speaks. "What a foolish, foolish thing to do. Can you imagine if Justin had broken his back? Or his neck?"

Of course I could imagine it; I've been imagining it all afternoon.

"You need to tell your parents about this," she says. "Not just about Justin, about everything."

I nod mutely, knowing she is right.

"You should come up with a game plan—not a game. I can give you a list of therapists to talk to or I'll be glad for the two of us to talk; whatever you're more comfortable with."

She places her hand on my arm. "Reaching out to people when we need help is one of the hardest things to do. No matter how old we are."

I nod, then lean across the counter to hug her. Her arms hold me stiffly; I can't say I blame her for being mad. We both walk down to Justin's room. He is fast asleep, covers strewn across the floor.

I sit next to him anyway, just watching his back rise and fall. I whisper a prayer under my breath—*PLEASE may he be okay. Please MAY he be okay. Please may HE be okay. Please may he BE okay. Please may he be OKAY.*

This horrendous, torturous day is almost over.

Yet I know this is only the beginning.

Please may *I* be okay.

"Monica had a breakdown! Monica had a breakdown!" Billy skips through the kitchen, singing, banging a spoon on the back of the colander.

My father grabs Billy by the arm and leads him to his room. He must have threatened him with no TV for a month because he stays put. Luckily Tish is at choir practice.

I told my mother the whole story when I first got back from Darcy's, but she wanted to have a "powwow" once Dad got home. She paged him at the office and told him to skip rehearsal tonight. She stopped by the toy store and picked up some Colorforms and videos for Justin, then apologized to Darcy fifty million times. My body is racked with guilt and I would rather pull out my entire set of teeth with rusty pliers than rehash the episode yet again.

"What were you thinking?" my father demands.

"You've always been so responsible," my mother adds.

"I know."

"The only thing we *know* is that a little boy might have permanent eye damage because of your negligence," my mother says.

"I would give him a transplant if I could," I mutter. (It's not like I've been seeing too clearly anyway.)

"Now explain this Game thing to me again," my father says.

Multiple Choice has made perfect sense to me during the past two weeks, although as I explain it now, my parents' faces are not filled with insight but confusion.

"Let me get this straight," my father says. "You picked a letter from your Scrabble game and that letter told you to lock Justin in his room? Is that right?"

I nod.

"Does that sound like a good game to you?" he asks.

"Um, no, that really wasn't a good choice."

"I should have paid closer attention when you tried to balance those beanbags," my mother says.

"Fixing those chairs wasn't part of the Game," I mutter.

"That almost makes it worse!" My mother looks as tired as I've ever seen her look. "So wearing pajamas to school, singing on the bus—were they choices too?"

I nod again.

"So you've been some kind of Scrabble robot these past few weeks, is that it? How are we supposed to help you, Mon, if you have this whole world going on in your head that you don't share with us?"

It's a good question that I don't have an answer to.

"You've got so much going for you," she continues. "Why on earth would you make up such a game?"

I try to come up with something that makes sense. "I wanted to stop obsessing."

"You're so bright, you've got so many friends," my father adds.

"No, I don't. Lynn and I aren't even friends anymore."

"You won that Model Student Award last year," my mother says.

"YOU'RE NOT EVEN LISTENING TO ME!" I shout.

The sound of my raised voice stuns them into silence. "Stop telling me how great my life is, how much I've got going for me. I'M MISERABLE! Haven't you figured that out yet?"

My mother stops frantically cleaning the kitchen and sits down. "You never said anything before."

"What was I supposed to say? That my mind is like a broken record? That I worry about making a mistake with every breath? That I invented Multiple Choice to take away the option of being wrong?"

"What the hell is she talking about?" Dad asks my mother.

"Why are you calling me 'she'? I'm right here!" I slide my back along the wall until I'm sitting on the floor.

My mother finally speaks. "We're not mind readers, Mon. Broken record or otherwise. You should have come to us for help."

"I just feel so much pressure," I say softly, into my sleeve.

"What does she have to feel pressure about?" my father asks. "You want to talk about pressure? Try a 2.4-million-dollar-a-year quota selling software nobody wants to buy. *That's* pressure."

My mother shoots him a look that shuts him right up. "You're at a tough age," she says. "I think Darcy's right; it's smart for you to talk to someone. Do you want me to call one of those therapists, do you want to see Ms. Mitchell, or would you rather talk to Darcy?"

If you add one more option, I think to myself, there'll be four and we can play Multiple Choice to decide. I almost smile at my own joke, but Mom would fling the waffle iron at me for even thinking about playing again. A, B, C. If I leave it to chance, I might get Ms. Mitchell, and the thought of placing my fragile psyche in her hands is enough to cure me overnight. I make the decision on my own and tell Mom I'll see Darcy. If she can ever get over being mad at me.

"I think that's a good idea," she says. "I'll call her in the morning."

My father is still baffled as he heads for the living room. "You know you can always talk to us, Mon. No matter what else is going on."

"Yes, Dad. I know."

I think I'm going to be sick.

★   ★   ★

My mother's still sitting at the table, staring out the rain-streaked window to our darkened backyard. Her body is here, but my mother seems far away. For the first time in fourteen years I've given her something to worry about. I almost feel bad for her, not having a perfect Monica anymore.

"You used to be so funny," she finally says. "My most flexible, easygoing baby."

This is news to me.

She gazes out at the backyard as if I am still a toddler on the swings. "You used to laugh at yourself all the time. I remember when you were three, three and a half, you had this pop-up book you loved. One day you were too rough with it and pulled off all the little flaps. A dog, a mouse, I don't remember what else. Most other kids would've cried that the book was ruined, but you laughed and laughed. You played with the little flap, saying, 'Doggie go for a walk now.' I swear, you loved the book more broken than you did new."

"Me? Are you sure?" Sounds more like Justin.

My mother nods, still staring outside at some long-ago toddler who eventually turned into a basket case.

I climb into my mother's lap—it's been ages. "I don't know what happened to that little girl," I say.

"It's a real downside to the job, but mothers always blame themselves," Mom replies. "I can't help thinking you stopped exploring the world and began to tame it because you thought it would be easier for me."

Mom and I have never talked like this before. I search for the right words to express what I'm really feeling. "You always had the three of us, plus the other kids. You were so happy and grateful when I helped."

"Oh, Mon. Who doesn't want their kids to be good? But I would have loved you even if you were a handful." She ekes out a smile. "I love your brother, don't I?"

Why is life so confusing? How did I end up in the worst trouble any of us have ever been in by trying to be perfect?

"It wasn't your job to be perfect and obedient and right all the time. It was your job to be you." She holds me tighter. I'm in an awkward position, but I don't want to move and stop her from hugging me. I stare down at her bare toes with the chipped wine nail polish.

When the phone rings, I can tell it's my grandpa and I scrunch my face with the fear that Mom will tell him about Justin. Thankfully, she chats about the craft fair instead.

I head out in the rain past the swing set, slides, and climbing structures, looking for the little girl my mother used to see out here. I open the door to the small gray castle and crawl inside. This castle is a favorite of the toddlers, with its orange slide and secret fireplace door.

Justin used to play in it for hours.

The rain picks up and is soon splashing off the turret onto my shirt and jeans. I think of the drawing of the "damp pirate" in my notebook. I don't want to be damp, or a pirate for that matter. Right now I want to get wet, really soaked, catch pneumonia, and die.

I trace the plastic bricks of the castle with my wet and wrinkled fingers. My hair, matted and soaked, hangs limply in front of my face. I suck one of the strands, flavorless as straw, and let the sports announcer have a field day. *My parents will never forgive me; they will fight even more than they normally do. They will finally get divorced because of me. They will have an ugly, brutal custody battle and Billy, Tish, and I will be split up and assigned to foster homes. Billy and Tish will have wonderful families they love and I will get some scary lady with hairs growing out of her moles. Billy and Tish will hate me for making my parents break up, so they won't see me for holidays, but I'll get presents in the mail from them—books I've already read and CDs I already own. On my birthday, I'll get a card signed with something fake like "warmly, Billy and Tish" and no one will love me, not even the lady with the hairy moles, because I am unlovable. . . .*

I let myself go on for a good half hour, wallowing down the dark paths of my mind. As nice as it would be to blame my mother or anybody else for my predicament, I know the responsibility falls squarely on me. For all my obsessing and planning, I'm completely at a loss for what to do.

How do you know when your life *really* begins? This thing I call a life now seems more like a bad dress rehearsal where none of the microphones work. When will it feel okay to really be *me*? I'm not leaving this castle until I figure out what to do, which means I might be out here for a while and pneumonia is a definite possibility.

Damsel in distress, that's me.

```
J R E E P L E H F G V H Y U
O K M N H Y T R E H S D V C
H Y U D C N B K I E U P L M
O E N V C D E R T L S Q B Y
L U L O I W P T S P E P A P
G Y T P X N V B Q P L M H L
G E W U I M B X R U G J W E
J H E L P M E S S A T Y U H
O K I U J H Y G T F R F D W
B V C X Z A S D F P L E H W
```

I devote myself to Justin's every waking need. I walk the path between our houses so often in the next week that the city workers might have to come and repave the sidewalks. I go to the library daily and take out the maximum amount of books. I spend the day reading them to Justin, then walk back to the library, return them, and take out a new stack. I make puppets from my favorite socks, I reenact *Flubber* (I bounce around the room so hard in my impersonation of Robin Williams that I bruise my left hip). I bake him brownies, whip up fruit shakes, and cut his peanut-butter-and-jelly sandwiches into stars with cookie cutters. Justin eats up the attention with a spoon.

"I'm really sorry," I tell him yet again.

"I fell out the window—bang!"

"Justin, do you hear me? I'm sorry."

"I'm sorry too." He smiles, then jumps on the bed, trying to touch the ceiling.

I also meet with Darcy when I visit. She doesn't make me lie on the couch like at some psychiatrist's office the way Billy said she would; we just talk for an hour in her kitchen. We talk about the trees I've been making, about how much I love word games, and what my plans are for the summer. (Besides getting over my guilt about Justin.) Our conversations make me realize how no one really listens when you talk. Darcy hangs on every word like I'm giving away the exact location of the Fountain of Youth. It makes me talk more, and more still. I can see why all those high school kids wanted her to stay.

"When I was in high school, you know what I obsessed about?" she asks.

Darcy—obsess? This I've got to hear.

"Food," she continues. "I thought about it all the time. Tried to force my will on it, tried to prove I was in control. For six months my senior year all I ate were grapefruit sections and diet soda. Spent most of my time lusting over chocolate and peanut butter but feeling I was better than other girls because I didn't give in to my cravings. I was in complete control until the day I passed out at my locker and woke up in the emergency room. All that acid eating away at my insides—I almost died." She shakes her head. "I was so isolated, so lonely. It took me years to make the connection."

"I'm not lonely," I say. But the word stings me as soon as I say it out loud, like a slap across the face.

"Lots of people are. Most kids your age spend their time wondering where they fit in."

"That's easy," I answer. "Nowhere."

"You know that's not true." She reaches across the counter for my arm.

"There's probably some name for this," I say. "Some sick diagnosis for people like me."

"I don't believe in labeling," she says. "I don't think it helps."

"Darcy, I'm so sorry." I feel the tears burning down my cheeks for the tenth time this week.

"I know you are, honey. Time to put it behind you."

She's right, of course, but I continue to cry anyway—about Justin, about Lynn, about my whole life. Darcy waits for me to finish.

"I just think too much," I finally say.

"You don't think enough," she answers. "Good thinking is never a problem, believe me."

"But . . ." My words trail off and I think about the toaster I wanted my mind to become. "Thinking's *always* been my problem."

"If you had been thinking, you wouldn't have locked Justin in his room; you wouldn't have written something bad about Lynn in the bathroom; you would have known that Monica was who you were supposed to be." She twirls her hair on top of her head and reaches for two pencils on the counter. "Stop thinking there's something wrong with your mind—there isn't. Just focus that wonderful brain of yours on different things."

"Like what?" What could possibly be more important

than fixating on Lynn hanging out with Christine now or that one strand of Darcy's hair the pencil didn't catch?

"What do you dream about being when you grow up?" Darcy asks.

I give my standard answer. "Maybe an English teacher."

"What else?"

"This is going to sound stupid," I say. "But sometimes I think about being a cryptographer. Do you know what that is?"

"Someone who deciphers codes. You'd be good at that!"

"I don't think there are too many available jobs," I say. "It's kind of a weird thing to want to be."

"Says who?" Darcy checks on Justin in his room, comes back down, and hands me a candy bar from the freezer. "There may be tons of companies looking for cryptographers. Maybe there's a whole new field now that everyone uses computers."

I imagine myself in front of a screenful of letters, finding combinations, moving them around, uncovering the secret code that saves the world.

"You should check that out," she says. "It's a perfect example of changing your focus."

Focus makes me think of focus wheel, which makes me think of my kaleidoscope, which Justin never uses and I miss terribly. Oh, well. I kiss him good-bye, thank Darcy, and head home. From the top of my street, I watch Lynn, Nicole, Christine, and Karen sunbathing in Lynn's yard. When I walk by, I try to decide if I should say hi, or just wave, or say nothing at all. I decide to really make an effort.

"Hi!"

Lynn and Karen lift their heads from their towels, then put them back down. Christine and Nicole don't even budge. Their silence echoes in my head like a gunshot.

Nothing too hard to decode there.

Tish has been great through all of this, unlike Billy, who covers his face with his hands like two shutters, then opens them, crosses his eyes, and says, "Cuckoo!" She spent the first day begging me to tell her the whole story, swearing on a stack of Bibles that she wouldn't tell anyone. After telling her for the millionth time that I don't want to talk about it, she finally gives up.

"Is there anything I can do?" she asks.

"Put me out of my misery like when we used to play with your horse dolls."

My father steps into the room as if he's onstage and we're the audience. "Alas! Who would like to accompany me to the local pet shop to appropriate some sustenance for our beloved Jethro?"

Tish and I look at each other, then at him. "No thanks."

"A most exceptional day has sprung forth from the loins of the gods. . . ."

I interrupt him. "Dad, really, I just want to stay home."

"I've got rehearsal at two," Tish says.

"Plenty of time, plenty of time!" He leads us to the car as if we're in a procession.

On the way to the pet store, he sings old show tunes in that loud opera voice we used to think was funny but is now just plain embarrassing. Tish and I roll our eyes so many times I'm afraid we might need to get glasses.

We load up the cart with two bags of dog food and a rawhide bone for a treat.

"Young maiden Monica." Dad holds his finger in the air like he's Shakespeare with an idea. "Perhaps a new friend would cheer you up?"

Perhaps an old friend. Perhaps Lynn.

He points to a tankful of goldfish. "What say ye to this fine orange fellow?"

"Dad, I don't want a goldfish. Last time we had one, he died the first night."

"And Jethro stuck his head in the toilet trying to eat him after we threw him away," Tish adds.

"Nonsense. It's an exceptional idea."

Dad's ideas to help me since Justin's accident have all been torture—working up a good sweat at the batting cages, getting a physical from Dr. Thompson to make sure I'm neurologically okay. But purchasing a fragile orange pet is by far the worst. I continue to tell him I don't want a goldfish, but he doesn't listen.

We watch the salesperson scoop up the fish, slip it into a plastic bag, then knot it.

"If Monica gets a new fish, what do I get?" Tish asks.

That was only a matter of time.

"How about a turtle?"Tish suggests.

Dad looks into the next tank. "A turtle it is!"

Tish runs down the aisle to find the salesperson again.

Whenever Dad changes from his acting voice to his normal voice in an instant, you know there's a lecture involved. "You need to take on a little more responsibility, young lady. That's your problem."

I don't want to make him mad by explaining that the goldfish won't be around long enough to teach me responsibility and besides, that isn't part of my problem anyway.

"I'm not afraid of responsibility." I swing the plastic bag like an aquarium purse.

"Good. Maybe we should get you a bird too."

"NO! Thanks, the fish is enough." How about a normal conversation? I think. I'll talk, you'll listen. Then you'll talk, I'll listen. Real radical stuff.

The woman hands Tish the turtle in a little box with holes in it. She gives us instructions on care and shows Dad the kind of tank we need.

"My turtle can eat your goldfish." Tish smiles sweetly. "But I won't let him."

Gee, thanks. What happens when we get home and Billy finds out we didn't get anything for him? Will Dad take him back here to buy an iguana? Yeah, right.

The woman at the cash register rings up item after item. "Mom's not going to like this," I say.

"Your mother *loves* animals."

Tish runs ahead to look at the Dalmatians.

"This is a step in the right direction," Dad says. He puts his arm around me. "I'm so glad we had this talk."

Since when does purchasing reptiles and soon-to-be-dead fish count as *talking*? I look inside the plastic bag—the poor fish already looks pale.

Tish calls the front seat on the way home.

"I feel better already. Don't you, Monica?" Dad says.

I lie across the backseat and cover my head with Jethro's blanket. "Can we just stop talking about this?" He's proud of himself, thinking he's done his part in my recovery. His cluelessness combined with the blanket on my head make me feel sick to my stomach as we pull out of the parking lot.

I hold the delicate bag against me and try to envision where we are. I picture the streets in my mind—left on Pine, right on Thurston—smiling as I think we're pulling into the driveway. But I'm off a bit and my father keeps driving. I feel like a kidnap victim trying to memorize the route to the hideout so she can find her way out and escape.

In a case of the worst-possible timing in the history of the world, my parent-teacher conference is scheduled for tonight. My father had a meeting in Phoenix he couldn't get out of, thank God. (Last year he slipped into that bad Shakespeare voice about a million times.)

My mother's been giving me pep talks all week— "Everyone has problems; you have so much going for you!" and my favorite, "You'll look back on this when you're older and really get a kick out of it." I almost wish she'd punish me instead. She called Mr. Bergeron to warn him that I'd been under a lot of stress lately. I begged her not to tell him about Multiple Choice. But her embarrassment succeeded more than my begging; she didn't.

"Monica loves English; she always has," Mom tells him. "She scrambles up words all the time with my father. I never have any idea what they're talking about. The word-game gene must have skipped a generation in our family."

I try to unscramble *family* into some other word, maybe one that makes me feel more at home. I go to take my seat, then move over a row and sit in Lynn's. It's probably the closest I'll come to hanging out with her anytime soon.

"Monica could have taught the section on figures of speech," Mr. Bergeron says. "She came up with more anagrams and oxymorons than I did."

Can we go home now? I trace my fingers along the spirals and numbers etched into the wood of Lynn's desk.

"I really don't have much else to say," Mr. Bergeron continues. "The only assignments that maybe—maybe— seem to give her any difficulty are the subjective ones. She's happier when there's a concrete answer."

Do we have to go into this? Ugh.

My mother glances my way with a nervous smile, and for a minute I think she's going to spill the beans to Mr. Bergeron. My face turns twenty shades of purple.

"Monica, what do you think?" Mr. Bergeron asks.

Monica? Monica left the building fifteen minutes ago, I want to say. Instead I answer quietly, "I try to do things the right way, that's all."

My mother beats the subject like a dusty rug on the clothesline. "She sits in front of a blank piece of paper for so long sometimes, I'm afraid she's getting hypnotized. Those assignments when you have to make up stories and use your imagination really make her uncomfortable."

Not any more than your little speech, I think. By the way, Mom, you forgot to tell Mr. Bergeron about the scab on my left elbow and how I used to eat bananas in my playpen.

Mr. Bergeron nods, then sits down beside me. "I've got an idea that worked well with a student last year."

I want to say, "Another perfectionist weirdo hypnotized by fright? Another girl thinking she can save the world by being perfect?" Instead I listen politely.

Mr. Bergeron takes a pad of paper and a pen from his desk. He scribbles across the borders of the paper with long, loopy squiggles, then rips the page from the pad and hands it to me. "From now on, I want you to doodle on the paper before you start your homework."

I try not to look too dumbfounded.

"That way, you don't have to worry about having perfect homework. Your page is imperfect before you start." His smile is too big, like he's trying to sell me a used car with a loose muffler.

My mother nudges me. She's wearing that angry/eager expression she's had pasted on her face since Justin got hurt. "I think it's a great idea. You have nowhere to go but up, right? No matter what you do."

"I don't get it," I say. "How will that help me think of the right answers?"

"The point isn't to get the correct answers," Mr. Bergeron says. "The point is to free yourself up to be wrong."

"So are you going to tell the rest of the class to do this too? Tell everyone the point of doing homework is to be wrong? To be messy and careless?" This would certainly free up Joey and Mike the Mosquito. I look toward the classroom door again. Because our parent-teacher appointments are in alphabetical order, Christine will be coming soon. The thought of her overhearing this conversation makes me dizzy with fear.

"Monica, everyone has different issues with learning. Some students need to spend more time on their study habits, some need to concentrate on retention, some need to work on stress."

That's me in the front row, the stress case. If Mr. Bergeron doesn't wrap up this meeting soon, he'll have no idea the kind of stress he'll be creating for me. I stare over Mr. Bergeron's head to the map of the world on the wall. Madagascar—yes, that's where I want to be right now. Those stupid teenage witches on TV—able to pop from one place to another with the twitch of a nose. Nothing like that ever works when you need it to.

I hear voices in the hall and decide to take things into my own hands. "Sounds like a good idea, Mr. Bergeron. I'll give it a try tomorrow." I take the scribbled paper and slip it into my folder. Mr. Bergeron and my mother give each other some secret we-know-better-than-she-does smile and say good-bye. I tap on Lynn's desk, a Morse code of reconciliation. 1, 2, 3, 1, 2, 3, 1.

When my mother and I leave the room, we bump smack into Christine and her father. He's wearing tortoiseshell glasses and talking into a cell phone. Christine flips through several flyers for different department stores downtown. No big deal for either of them, just another meeting crammed into their busy schedules. I rub my thumb against the cuticles of my right hand. I have bitten and chewed them until they are red and raw, worried about this meeting. Looking at Christine so carefree makes me wonder if I really *am* the smartest person in the class.

Christine looks up from the ads to give me a smirk that says, "You may think you're so smart, but we both know you've lost your best friend." I hurry away while my mother babbles about Mr. Bergeron and his progressive ideas for learning. But her words are lost in the echo of the now empty hall. I tell her I have to use the bathroom, and she waits outside while I go in. I lock myself in the stall—a new one, not the one Lynn wrote in—and take the scribbled paper from my folder. I rip it up, wishing I had the wire cutters from my tool kit. I toss the fragments into the toilet.

Doesn't anyone understand that telling me I'm stressed all the time is *making* me stressed? And that being stressed is what drove me to Multiple Choice in the first place? I wipe my tears with a ribbon of toilet paper, then flush the whole insulting mess away.

Here are some of the things I've been thinking about:

I want to take all the baby-sitting money I have saved during the past two years, go to Toys "R" Us, and buy every game of Scrabble they have on the shelf. Then I want to make the clerk go into the back room and bring out every game of Scrabble waiting to be shelved. I want to buy them, take them home, and lock the door to my bedroom. I rip open the plastic bags containing the letters, dump them on my floor, and make a huge pile, bigger than the pile of leaves under our maple tree in October. Then I want to plop in the middle of the tiles, cover myself with them, pour them on my head like an alphabetical shower—J, D, Z, E, R, I, T. I want them to rain on me, pour on me, until sooner or later, some words, some idea will begin to form from them and magically—or maybe through some kind of phonetic osmosis—an idea will begin to form in my head. Then I drag out the vacuum from the hall closet and vacuum them away, letting the suction scoop up the letters from my life one by one.

Better yet . . . *I go outside after dinner while the coals of the gas grill are still hot. Billy and Tish will be cleaning up and Mom won't notice I'm outside alone. I drop the letters through the grates and they melt on the white-hot coals—E, M, F, L, J, O—thousands of years of meaning and sound melting like bits of fat from a piece of chicken. I drop every letter in until they are indistinguishable. A pile of gray ash blowing around the backyard like some alphabetical cremation.*

Or this . . .

Because of the noise factor, I wait until Mom's not home, then fill up the blender with a few ice cubes and some water. It's one of those industrial blenders Dad brought home during one of his "let's get healthy" stages. I drop the Scrabble tiles in one by one. The blades crunch but don't break with the burden. P, N, B, V, E, C plop into the pulpy liquid. After all the letters are inside, I lift the blender from its base and head to the garden. I pour the frothy alphabet onto the fertile soil and wonder if the wood contains any special vitamins or minerals that will help the vegetables grow. Maybe in a few months, our zucchini and tomatoes will be extra tasty—or maybe they'll just have a good vocabulary.

But it's not the letters' fault, or even the Scrabble tiles'. I got myself into this; I have to get myself out, one baby step at a time. It just seems like so much WORK. Darcy's given me daily tasks to work toward. She says taking small steps almost guarantees success, that big overnight changes like New Year's resolutions or Multiple Choice usually fizzle out or come crashing down. Today's assignment is to open my locker without spinning the lock three times.

I haven't felt as much fear at my locker since the day I stood there deciding whether to take off my raincoat and show off my pajamas. To just turn the lock without clearing it, without wiping away all traces of past mistakes seems like a surefire way to ask for disaster. I remind myself that nothing terrible happened when I didn't cut my sandwich in quarters or didn't wear my blue socks for Monday's math test. I spin the dial, open my locker, and take out my history book. There.

The rest of the day isn't great, but the world doesn't collapse either. Like that astronaut said, "One small step for a girl, one giant leap for mankind."

Something like that anyway.

Darcy only gave me one assignment for today, but there's been one I've been meaning to do that I've put off long enough. Several weeks ago, I asked the letters if I should tell Lynn about Multiple Choice. The answer was no, for as long as I played the game. Well, Multiple Choice is over now, so I won't be breaking any of the Ground Rules. Besides, I've got nothing left to lose.

I corner Lynn at her locker. My heart is beating so loud I can barely hear, but I plunge ahead anyway. "Got a new fish. Named him X. Only a matter of time before he's gone."

"I don't really care," she answers.

I tell myself to quit stalling. I take a big breath and tell her everything about Multiple Choice. I don't even care if she tells Christine; I owe it to Lynn.

"Can't you see? I didn't have a choice about what I wrote." My voice is hopefully upbeat.

She looks at me like I'm asking for directions to Afghanistan.

"You *had* a choice," she says. "You could have chosen not to put trashing me as an option. Or you could have chosen not to do it."

"See, that's the thing. I *didn't* have a choice. That was the *point.*"

"The *point* is that you chose something you knew would hurt me and you did it anyway. That's the point."

I try to remain patient. "You don't understand."

"No, *you* don't understand. You were mean. You were cruel. I can't believe you come to me with this lame excuse that you were some kind of alphabet zombie and I'm supposed to say okay and be friends again."

"I was wrong," I say. "I've apologized a million times. I went to the office supply store to see if they had any stuff that removes permanent ink."

"Yeah, so you could erase what I wrote about *you.*"

"No! I mean, I would have done that too, but that's not why. I *miss* you. You're my best friend."

"Nicole and I are best friends now."

Hearing that sentence out loud is almost as painful as hearing the crash in Justin's room. I swallow my pride even further. "Maybe the three of us can do something sometime."

"I'm sorry, Monica. I really am."

She closes her locker and heads down the hall. What do

they call it when people have a leg amputated and still feel it? A phantom limb, something like that? That's what my friendship with Lynn is—something I loved for so long, but it just isn't there anymore. Maybe I'll get used to it. Or maybe I'll feel it sometimes late at night, a burning sensation waiting to be scratched, reminding me of my loss.

This afternoon my mother's watching Justin while Darcy and I go to the woods. "You've made such a connection with trees," she says. "We should take advantage of that."

I'm just glad her frostiness from that first day has thawed. We walk along in silence until Darcy points to the trail with the blue marker. I follow her.

She doesn't waste any time once we're on the trail. "You said it was important for you not to be wrong, how your body used to fill with fear."

I'm grateful she uses the past tense, as if we are analyzing someone else, as if I am cured. "*Why* was I like that?" I ask.

She shakes her head. "It doesn't matter why—something a teacher once said, your parents' or your own expectations, some bad spinach you ate as a kid. All of it's ancient history. Let's just concentrate on feeling your feelings now."

I heave a huge sigh of relief. I'd filled three notebook pages with a list of why I'm so obsessive (although the spinach idea never occurred to me). None of the reasons got me any closer to feeling better.

Darcy sits on a stump and points to my pack. "Let's have a juice. And while you're in there, take out that notebook."

I've never let anyone go through my notebook before. She must see my hesitation because she doesn't push. "Are you sure?" she asks when I hand it to her.

I nod.

She skims through the pages. "Didn't you make a list of your good qualities? Ah, here it is. Reliable, intelligent, dependable. That's it?"

I shrug. Even they don't seem too applicable after Justin's injury.

She takes the pen from the spiral binding. "Okay, twenty more. Let's go."

"Twenty? No way." I pause. "Maybe one or two."

"Modest, good. We'll start with that. What else?"

"Ummm."

She waits, then fills the silence. "Creative—those trees are proof of that. Fit—you climbed up that hill without a gasp. Helpful—your mother couldn't run her business without you. Polite—Justin's manners are much better since you've been baby-sitting. There's four; now your turn."

I think about how many times I stuck with Multiple Choice even when I knew it was wrong. "Stubborn?"

"Let's call it persistent."

I inch my way through more good qualities—ambitious, organized—until the page is filled.

Darcy stands and heads farther up the trail. "Twenty strengths, twenty flaws. Twenty-twenty," Darcy continues.

"Balance is important." She stops at a fallen tree, a huge pine on the right side of the trail. The broken trunk lies about ten feet off the ground. She climbs on and walks slowly across the tree. I hold my breath until she reaches the other side. She finally does, then climbs down.

"Your turn."

"Me? No way. This is harder than the balance beam at school."

"And no cliquey girls making fun of you when you fall." She extends her hand.

"I really don't want to."

"Of course you don't—you're full of fear. That's what we've been talking about all week. Let's go. I'm right here to catch you if you fall."

I tell Darcy I'm going to get sick. She tells me to go ahead, that there's a towel in the pack. She guides me to the giant stump and I place one foot on the massive trunk.

"Pretend you're from a long line of acrobats," she says. "Hey, your father's an actor, right? Maybe there's some circus performer in your genes."

The thought of some ancestor in a leotard holding a giant stick to balance herself as she slides along the high wire does not reassure me. My gaze travels from my feet to the end of the trunk, trying to find a good point to fix on.

"Good job! You're doing it!" Darcy walks alongside me.

Only a few more feet . . . I stumble, grab onto a branch to catch myself. Another few minutes and I reach the end. The back of my T-shirt is soaked with sweat.

Darcy helps me off and we jump up and down on the moss. "You did it!" she shouts.

I pound my chest like Tarzan, pretty damn proud.

Darcy walks me back a few feet to view my accomplishment. "I bet you never thought you'd be able to do it."

"Never."

She takes out her pen. "I guess we have to add 'brave' and 'daring' to the list."

"Don't forget 'good balance,' " I add.

"Balance, that's what it's all about, Monica."

We head out and I turn several times to look at the tree. It was high! My victory fills me with giggles, and we laugh all the way back to the car. As soon as I begin to wonder how today's lesson ties in with Multiple Choice, Darcy reads my thoughts.

"Don't give up taking chances," Darcy says. "That's what life is made of. But listen to your feelings, whatever they are. If you let yourself feel them, you don't have to obsess about them."

She swats a mosquito. "God, that's enough talking from *me* today. Much more fun walking on trees."

And for the first time since Justin's accident, I feel alive. This DOES count.

★

★ ★ ★

★ ★ ★ ★ ★ ★

Germinate a skim

Migrate me a skink

Angie met a smirk

Me stink a mirage

Grease a mink, Tim

Rim me in a gasket

Kim, I'm a sergeant

A knit miser game

I ★★★ am ★★★ making ★★★ trees

Mom and I walk over to Grandpa's to bring a few groceries and some audiotapes from the library. She feels bad that my fish died—surprise!—so she buys us ice-cream cones on the way. It's not even technically summer yet, but the heat's already starting to get to Jethro. He's been lying around the yard for days, so I take him with us for some exercise.

"Darcy gave me some articles to read," Mom says. "They were very informative."

I picture myself as a case study in some psychology journal and almost trip on the curb. Mom tells me that lots of girls my age get obsessed with controlling their environment and trying to be perfect. I tell her about the conversation I had with Darcy yesterday about girls being people pleasers. "Darcy says it's important not to give up your own power."

"Power? Who do you know with any power? I change kids' poops all day—and they're not even my kids!" She shakes her head, and I blame myself for derailing the conversation. Too much touchy-feely stuff always loses my mother.

I guess I don't give her enough credit because she bounces right back. "But if she's telling you it's more important to spend your life pleasing yourself than pleasing others, she's right." She rings the buzzer to Grandpa's apartment with conviction.

He opens the door with his usual grin. "NO INCOME."

"NICE MOON," I reply.

"I will never for the life of me figure out these word games," Mom says.

I lead Jethro in while Mom puts down the bag of groceries. My grandfather gives her a wink. "NO INCOME, NICE MOON, COME ON IN."

I play cards with Grandpa while Mom puts the groceries away and picks up. She asks him about his friends at the coffee shop and how Mrs. Clemente next door is doing with her broken wrist. When she opens the linen closet to put the toothpaste away, she turns to face Grandpa with her hands on her hips.

"Dad, what are you doing with all these Q-tips?" She takes the boxes out of the closet one by one and lines them on the counter. Like one of those tiny cars that a hundred clowns climb out of, the Q-tips seem to be multiplying inside the linen closet.

I jump up from the table and begin to count. "Thirty-seven boxes!"

My grandfather's eyes twinkle like a naughty boy who's been caught eating before dinner. "They were on sale."

"You won't live long enough to clean your ears this much. *I* won't live long enough to clean my ears this much."

I worry that she's hurt his feelings, but when I look over, he's laughing too. "I got a little carried away." He's on a roll now and opens the cupboard next to the sink. He takes out stacks and stacks of green plastic baskets.

"What came in these, strawberries?" I ask.

"Blueberries too." He continues to remove them from the cupboard. There are so many covering the floor, Jethro begins to bark.

"Ninety-six little crates! Mom, look! What are you going to do with them?"

"Oh, I don't know," he answers. "Seemed wasteful to throw them away."

I giggle with him, partly because the floor looks like a giant green lattice maze and partly because I understand how easy it is to get carried away with something, especially something that makes no sense. I love my grandpa's reaction—laughing at himself along with Mom and me. It makes me see how seriously I've been taking myself all this time.

"You can probably glue them together and make a life-size replica of the Eiffel Tower," my mother says.

"Let's do it!" I shout. "It'll make a great summer project."

"The two of you," she says. "Two peas in a pod."

"IOWA POND PASTE," we answer in unison.

She shakes her head. "I give up."

My grandfather roars with laughter. "Two peas in a pod" is one we've done together many times. Poor Mom thinks we're in some special club she can't get into.

While Grandpa and I stack the cartons by the door, Mom stands at the stove and stirs a can of tomato soup. "I just decided something," she says. "I'm going to take August off."

I am shocked. "You haven't taken a vacation, ever."

"I know. It's about time."

I immediately think it's because she's worried about me—she wants to monitor my progress, make sure I don't spend the summer obsessing over things like the backyard structures leaving dead spots in the grass. I gather up my courage and pull her aside. "Mom? Is it because of me?"

"Monica, I hate to tell you this, but you are *not* the cause of every little thing that happens in the universe. The fate of the free world does *not* rest on your shoulders."

Whew.

"Maybe I'm exhausted and ready for a long overdue vacation." She's wearing a huge smile and her eyes are twinkling almost as much as Grandpa's. "Maybe it's time to stop changing diapers for a while and start going to the beach." She pretends to dive into the invisible ocean of the kitchen, causing Jethro to bark even more.

My mind begins to race—*What if the parents of the kids get really mad that she's taking time off? And what if they all find another day care place to go to in the fall? What if it's September and Mom's sitting on the seesaw in the backyard by herself and no one shows up?* I switch stations in my head and remember Darcy telling me to focus on something positive. So I focus on my mother riding the waves to shore, enjoying her well-deserved vacation.

I jump into the pretend ocean of the kitchen and grab my mother's hands; Grandpa does too. Soon the three of us are twirling around the kitchen, leaning back, the tension between us keeping us in balance. And I feel "normal" right now, spinning around with my kowabunga mother and Q-tips-hoarding grandpa. I don't know why I've spent so much time obsessing about not being perfect—other people's imperfections seem to be the most interesting things about them. Maybe about me too.

Jethro's on his hind legs, jumping near the counter. I figure he wants to join us, so I hold his paws like we're dancing. He ignores me and goes for the tomato soup now cooling in the bowl. Maybe there's room in life for some surprises after all.

Dad's the one in the play, but the rest of us are nervous. (Making us wear our best clothes only adds to the tension.) The theater is in the basement of a church three towns away. Dad left earlier for "one last run-through."

After we take our seats, Tish grabs my sleeve. "I wish Daddy did this for a real job, don't you? Maybe even be in the movies." Tish's vision of the world is so different from mine; for her, anything is possible. I have always just concentrated on getting through the day without calling any attention to myself—and look where that got me. Maybe things are changing, though; I read some interesting articles this week about being a cryptographer— who knows what will happen if I apply my thousand-horsepower mind to it?

The curtain goes up and the room falls silent. The play is about a salesman and his wife and two sons. When my father comes out in the first scene, everyone applauds. (He is a real professional and keeps going, not acknowledging us.) Between the makeup and the stooped posture, Dad's almost unrecognizable.

Throughout the performance I catch myself clutching

the arms of the wooden chair. Suppose Dad flubs a line? Suppose he forgets what he's supposed to say and the play comes to a grinding halt? During intermission we can't see Dad, so the four of us have sodas in the lobby and talk about how great he was. Mom tells us the woman playing his wife is a hairdresser from Billerica with four kids. She looks so proud of Dad, and I imagine that's how she looked when she met him. She tells us the story again—he was playing Romeo in summer stock in her town. It must have been all the practice from the play, because she said he was so romantic, she knew she was going to marry him on their first date. Billy rolls his eyes and goes back to his seat, but Tish and I stay to hear about the floating orchids he sent to her office every day his theater group was in town.

The lights blink on and off to tell us to return to our seats, but all I can think of is Lynn's father calling her back home with his neighborhood signal.

The sadness of the play fills the basement of the church like incense. The two grown sons are unhappy failures and their father—*my* father—looks back on his life in despair. I try to blink back the tears but finally can't stop them. I know these are characters in a play, not real people, but their sadness and emptiness echo inside me like a ruin. The character Dad creates tonight is full of fear, a man not afraid of death, but of life. And I realize that I don't want to be empty and afraid anymore. That I'm tired of carrying these feelings around like a salesman with a briefcase.

When the salesman's wife stands at his graveside at the

end of the play, Billy, Tish, and I stiffen in our seats. Dad's not dead, of course, but it seems strange to have his character gone. The cast comes out at the end of the play and we applaud wildly, relieved to see Dad onstage again. The actors bow together several times, then each actor bows alone. When it's Dad's turn, we hoot and holler. The strange part is, everyone else does too. I guess he must have been pretty good.

Backstage is really the hallway, but it's decorated with streamers and there's a table full of food. My mother talks to my father's wife in the play, but I stay close to my father. He's removed his makeup and looks like normal Dad again.

"You seemed moved." Thankfully, he uses his normal voice.

"It's a very sad story," I answer.

"They should have shown you drive the car off the road," Billy says. "CRASH!"

Tish nudges him to be quiet, and Billy actually seems a little embarrassed. Maybe he should wear a tie more often.

"Weren't you worried you would make a mistake?" I ask.

"Made two of 'em. No one seemed to notice."

I nearly choke on my carrot stick. "What? You made two mistakes?"

"Acting's like real life, Mon. You make a mistake, you keep going. Everyone adapts. It's no big deal." He hurries to say hello to Mr. Jurzek while I stand in the wake of his words.

He made a mistake in front of hundreds of people and he doesn't even care? Better yet, no one even noticed? How is it possible that Dad got to me more as a fictional character than he ever has as a father? Maybe he should concentrate on what he loves to do rather than orchestrating lame heart-to-heart talks in pet stores. I smile across the room at him and he gives a goofy wave back. I guess he's just muddling through like the rest of us.

Mom gives Mr. Jurzek her camera to take a family picture. Billy doesn't put his fingers behind our heads like he usually does, and we all say "cheese." Mr. Jurzek hands me the picture and I watch the five of us appear as if by magic—our images slowly, surely edging their way out of the darkness.

D	I	F	F	E	R	E	N	T	P	O	S	D
R	T	S	F	Z	C	B	V	H	U	E	E	J
W	S	F	H	L	N	B	W	O	C	Z	D	E
I	K	L	M	N	J	V	W	I	M	A	O	T
G	O	U	B	L	X	Q	O	P	L	A	Q	S
I	T	G	C	X	Z	H	C	D	R	E	S	I
Y	T	B	M	N	C	E	U	O	P	L	M	N
T	R	E	D	F	H	B	V	C	X	W	E	Q
S	J	U	R	M	V	N	X	H	W	H	G	X
H	B	V	Q	N	M	U	E	Y	T	P	O	C

I hate to admit it, but there's a part of me that *misses* Multiple Choice. As catastrophic as it was to my life, I miss carefully making up the four choices, the anticipation before I chose the winning letter, the nervous excitement of walking out the door to do something strange and new. Darcy says I can skip the first two steps and still decide to do new things whenever I want to. She says doing that is what makes life interesting, that Multiple Choice was just a crutch, that I can have that same power whenever I want in *real* life. I'm not so sure.

But I *have* been feeling an itch to do something fresh and unexpected. Maybe some of my father's acting genes got passed on to me after all. I decide to make a present for Justin. I scan the house for ideas. In the day care playroom, I find everything I need—paper, markers, glitter. I stop at the pharmacy on the way to Justin's for the finishing touch.

Naked Justin squeals with delight when he sees me. "Ahoy, matey!"

When Darcy sees me enter the house wearing *my* eye patch, she claps and laughs too.

"If Justin wears one, *I* wear one." I feel totally conspicuous and stupid, of course, but in some strange way, the patch is a relief, like a surrender flag signaling that I've given up. The pharmacist didn't even blink an eye when I bought it (no pun intended).

"If you're not careful, you two will start a whole new trend," Darcy says.

I lift the patch to really look at her, wanting to see if she is mad. Her face is as kind and gentle as it's always been, for which I am grateful.

"I made you some presents," I tell Justin. He yanks on my pack to get a look. I pull out a red bandanna and tie it around his head. Then I slowly take out the item I spent all morning working on—a map.

"Buried treasure!" he yells. He jumps up and down, then shows the map to Darcy.

"You've done quite a job here. Burning the edges, weathering the paper. It's really quite beautiful," Darcy says.

I tell Darcy it's not as good as it could have been, that it would have been better with parchment but all we had at home was construction paper.

She lets me finish babbling. "Say, 'It's fine,' " she commands.

I look at the map, and it really is okay. "It's fine," I answer. We both smile.

The map leads to a treasure I just hid in the woodpile behind Darcy's garage—a box I decorated with gold wrapping paper and filled with beads and Christmas garland.

"X marks the spot!" Justin yells. "Let's go!"

"Don't you want to put your clothes on?" Darcy asks.

Justin looks down at himself and shakes his head no. Darcy shrugs.

"Looks like you're stuck with a naked pirate," she says. She leans in close to me and lifts up my eye patch. "Thanks for doing this for him. But you know you don't have to wear the eye patch, right?" She pauses. "You did this of your own free will—no Multiple Choice or anything?"

I look at her and answer honestly. "I just thought it would be fun."

She grins and puts the patch back in place. "Better go find that treasure."

I run outside after Justin, who is counting out the number of steps from the back door to the swing set. Little did I know when I drew the picture of the pirate in my notebook in Ms. Emerson's class over a month ago that *I'd* be wearing an eye patch, searching for buried treasure. Maybe when I get home, I can figure out some new anagrams for DAMP PIRATE besides I AM TRAPPED. Something like, I DON'T FEEL LIKE BEING TRAPPED ANYMORE, THANK YOU VERY MUCH.

My personal notebook is filled to the brim. I've gone back and used double sides, even margins, and I can't fit anything into it. I flip through the pages of word games, puzzles, and come to the Helpful Hints.

- **Don't Worry About What Other People Think.**
- **Be With Loved Ones. Take Advantage of Their Support.**
- **Keep Busy.**
- **Be Spontaneous.**

In some strange way, these tips have helped. I didn't worry about what people thought when I walked over to Justin's with the eye patch. I *am* having more fun being with my family. I have been pretty busy with the craft fair. And little by little, I am trying to be more spontaneous. (I took Webster Street instead of my usual Thurston today.) But why didn't these Helpful Hints work the first time? If they had, I never would have had to invent Multiple Choice, Justin wouldn't be hurt, Lynn and I would still be best friends, etc., etc., etc. Why did these tips only work *after* Multiple Choice?

Who knows? Maybe *I* made the difference; maybe *I've* changed. Maybe I'm not so locked into one way of thinking. Or maybe Multiple Choice was just something I had to do, some fire to walk through to get to the other side. All this thinking exhausts me and I close my notebook. I should throw it away—it's full, after all. But I open my desk drawer and place it gently inside. Where my kaleidoscope used to be, where my velvet bag of tiles used to be. I close the drawer and go outside.

Billy and Tish are drawing an elaborate maze on the driveway. I grab the orange stick of chalk and continue Tish's green line.

"Do you still want to make an Eiffel Tower with all those crates?" Billy asks. "We can make an unbelievable space station."

"Grandpa has enough crates for the Eiffel Tower, the Great Wall of China, and ten space stations," I answer.

We talk about how excited Mom is about vacation, how she cut out the calendar of the town's free concerts in the park and bought herself a big floppy straw hat. Billy puts the finishing touches on the maze and signs his full name with a flourish. I take my chalk and cross out letters one at a time, rearranging them on the driveway.

"WILLIAM DEVON," I say. "MINI-VOWEL LAD."

"Do another," Billy says. "A good one."

I rearrange the letters, chalk dust covering my fingers. After a few more minutes I come up with I, WALDO MELVIN and MO WILL INVADE.

"That's a good one!" He jumps up, climbs the porch railing, and proclaims to the entire neighborhood, "Watch out! Mo will invade! Get out your guns—Mo will invade!" He jumps off the porch. "Do another one."

Tish moves the letters, her green chalk intersecting mine. "How about I MOW EVIL LAND?"

"Excellent! I'll sing that when Dad makes me cut the grass." He paces the front yard, pushing an invisible lawn mower. "I mow evil land!"

Tish writes her own name on the driveway, then crosses it off. "It'll be better if I use my full name, right?"

I nod. She writes PATRICIA DEVON in block letters, then goes to work. "This is hard," she says. "How do you and Grandpa do it so fast?"

"Practice."

After a while, she comes up with a good first attempt. I TORN A CAP DIVE.

She continues to shuffle the letters. "Oh, too bad! I can make ACID RAIN, but then I have VETPO left over."

"I know. It's frustrating when you can almost do something great." I work with her until we come up with others. EVICT PARANOID, DRIVE TO A PANIC, and ION CADAVER PIT.

"I want that one," Billy yells.

"Then go change your name," I answer.

I whisper to Tish when I find a new one. "What happens when you sing outside in the rain? I DRIP AN OCTAVE."

Tish rolls on the driveway and laughs, her T-shirt now covered with a rainbow of chalk. "I'll remember that next time we have an outdoor series." She grabs my arm. "Help me find more."

I don't tell Tish I found another singing reference—A DARN PIT VOICE—because I wouldn't want to jinx her concert Saturday night. We work until Mom calls us for dinner.

Billy and Tish tell Mom what anagrams they've come up with. "Not more word games," she says. I feel my back tense as if I've done something wrong, as if she thinks I'm playing Multiple Choice again.

"I've got to get with the program. I'm beginning to feel left out." Mom puts down the plate of burgers and laughs. As I eat, I realize my fear of getting in trouble is half imagined and something I'll be working on for a while.

"I'M LOW AND EVIL!" Billy says for the fiftieth time. He actually came up with that one himself. He tosses me his pickle. "Here, Mon."

And it's just like that time in the diner last month except I'm being me, not a Multiple Choice creation. And surprise, surprise. Everyone likes me more.

My Favorite Anagrams of All Time
(I've been saving them for years)

- THE MORSE CODE—HERE COME DOTS
- UNITED STATES HISTORY—DATES UNITE THIS STORY
- HIBERNATES—THE BEAR'S IN
- THE ANSWER—WASN'T HERE
- A DECIMAL POINT—I'M A DOT IN PLACE
- THE COUNTRYSIDE—NO CITY DUST HERE
- ASTRONOMERS—MOON STARERS
- PRECAUTION—I PUT ON CARE
- THE PUBLIC ART GALLERIES—LARGE PICTURE HALLS, I BET
- VACATION TIMES—I'M NOT AS ACTIVE
- A STICK OF CHEWING GUM—THING OF MAGIC WE SUCK
- THE FRONTIERSMAN—HE TENTS ON FAR RIM

OW! A BREATHY TONE

becomes

A TWO-BEAN THEORY

becomes

BENEATH A ROW TOY

becomes

WET A NEARBY HOOT

becomes

OOH! A BARE TWENTY

becomes

OW! A TORN EYE BATH

becomes

ANOTHER WAY TO BE

On the way to the craft fair, my grandfather beams more than the headlights. The trunk is filled with fifteen different trees I have made. Ms. Cotter said they were innovative and intuitive, that I have a knack for working with my hands. It's the first time I have ever been complimented for anything creative. It feels good.

"Hark! A scrumptious feast for the eyes!" My father claps like this is the *Hamlet* of craft fairs. At first Mom and Grandpa were going to take me, but Dad wanted to come, so he canceled an appointment in Portland and came back early. Mom gave us each ten dollars to buy ourselves an end-of-the-school-year present. Tish races toward the beads and Billy rushes to the drums. After Grandpa, Mom, and Dad help me set up the table, they go to the cafeteria for some tea. Grandpa's so excited, he keeps wiping his forehead with his handkerchief.

Before the fair begins, I make the rounds. Marjorie from the other eighth-grade class made tiny stained-glass key chains, Bruce Thomas made CD holders from fruit crates. I barely make it through all the tables before the doors open and people start coming in. I take a seat next to my table, but the terror of being made fun of surrounds me almost to the point of suffocation. I take a deep breath and try to calm down.

When I see Darcy, a huge smile spreads across my face. She has been so kind and helpful over the past month; I finally understand how Justin can trust there will always be another ice-cream cone.

She raises her hands over her head when she sees the table of trees. "They're wonderful. All different, yet a piece of you. See how that works?" She gives me a giant hug.

"Is Justin okay?"

"He's with my mother. When I left, he had strapped two rags to his feet and was helping her wash the kitchen floor." She leans in close and whispers, "We saw Dr. Davis today. Justin has to keep the patch on, but I think he's going to be okay."

My sigh of relief can almost be heard in Toronto. "I'm so glad!"

"I am too." Darcy picks up a tree in the back row. "This one is just amazing. I'll take it." But when she reaches for her wallet, I jump up from my chair.

"No way. Take it. Please, as a gift."

She sits me back down and hands me twenty dollars. "I insist. You owe me nothing—just let your mistakes serve their purpose, okay?"

I argue with her for a few more minutes, but she insists. I place the tree gently in a box.

Before she leaves, she leans toward me and hands me my

eye patch. "You left this at the house the other day." Then she hands me a little package wrapped in delicate paint-splattered paper. "This is for you too."

I protest, but she puts her finger on her mouth as if to quiet me. I gently unwrap the small box. Inside is my kaleidoscope.

"He never uses it. It's silly for him to keep it."

"Darcy, I can't."

"Of course you can. But I'm afraid he didn't take good care of it. A few pieces of glass are loose."

I pause, knowing that I had promised never to look in the kaleidoscope again. That even through the terror of Justin's fall, I have not broken any Ground Rules. I hold the box tightly in my hand. "Thanks a lot," I say.

"Ooh, chopsticks." She heads to the next table, where Marie Bartlett is selling hair accessories. "Good luck, Mon," Darcy calls over her shoulder.

My good feelings are short-lived, however, when Christine and Karen approach the table. My stomach does a series of somersaults.

They browse the rows of trees. Christine picks up one from the back. Maybe she can tell me how badly I sing again.

"You made these?" she asks.

I nod, not wanting to say anything stupid.

"What are they?" Karen asks.

"They're trees."

"Duh," Christine says. "She was just wondering if you used them for something."

"They're earring holders." Outside of Multiple Choice, this is the first spontaneous thing I have ever said in my life.

Christine and Karen look at each other and nod approvingly. "Nice job," Karen says.

The old announcer voice inside me starts in. *Say something smart; don't screw up. This is a good first step; don't wreck it.* For a moment I am paralyzed with fear. I ignore the old voice inside me and answer from a place that is real and still afraid. "I wasn't sure anyone would like them."

"They're nice," Christine says. "Different." She and Karen move on.

Like a tightrope walker who makes it to the other side, I sigh and feel my ever present fear dismantle just a little.

My relief doesn't last long; Lynn is right behind them.

"Saw your grandpa," she says.

"Yeah, he's in his glory."

"I told him to check out the next row. Chris Keene is selling those Jesus night-lights again." Lynn looks at my field of trees. "These came out great."

"Thanks a lot." Here goes. "Do you want to come over later? My mother's making such a big deal out of this, she baked a cake and everything. . . ."

"Sorry, I can't." She's wearing the shirt I gave her for her birthday last year. Back when we were best friends. "Good luck."

"Thanks," I answer. "Have fun."

I feel a hand on my shoulder. It's my mother.

"How long have you been standing there?" I ask.

"Just got here. How's Lynn?"

"All right, I guess."

She squeezes my shoulder. "EWWO."

"What?"

"EWWO. Everything will work out." She gives me a wink. "You think you kids and Grandpa are the only ones who can make anagrams?"

Poor Mom, good at so many things—word games not being one of them. I want to tell her that EWWO is an acronym, not an anagram, but she's trying so hard to connect that I smile and tell her she'll be outfoxing Grandpa in no time.

"Do you think your father would like one of those wooden tie racks for his birthday?" she asks. "His ties keep falling off the old one."

I tell her yes and she heads down the aisle.

My father approaches from the other direction. "Dost thou think that fair maiden desires some—"

"Dad? Can you not be so weird tonight, PLEASE?"

He tries again. "Think your mother would like a pair of those beaded earrings?"

"With the necklace to go with it," I answer.

"You want me to drum up a little traffic, get people over here?"

"NO! I mean, thanks a lot, but it's okay."

"Never mind, you do your thing." He salutes and heads to the jewelry table.

Several people come by and most of them like the trees.

As the night goes on, I feel a little more relaxed and end up selling five of them.

I glance at the box from Darcy on the table. I tell myself I'm a different person now; I don't have to live by those Ground Rules anymore. I can set my own rules to follow.

I pick up the box and remove the kaleidoscope. I put the brass cylinder up to my eye and break my own rule, as clearly as if I had picked the letter C and ignored it. Darcy was right—the kaleidoscope *is* broken. As I turn the focus wheel, two yellow pieces between the red and blue triangles tumble inside, looking for a place to land, safe from their own jagged edges. I twirl the outer ring and watch them float among the other shapes, fixed and nonmoving. I suddenly love the kaleidoscope more than ever, love it for its imperfections. And for a minute, the little girl who loved the broken flaps in the pop-up book is alive and well, laughing and running through the backyard like a cheetah, not worrying about making mistakes, not figuring out a way to be perfect.

I start to put the eye patch in my pocket but slip it on one more time. I turn toward the ceiling light and look into the kaleidoscope again—one eye pitch-black, the other filled with a world of color. Both my eyes are covered, but I feel like I'm seeing clearly.

There's probably a great oxymoron in there somewhere.

It's the last week of school, so Mr. Bergeron takes us to the media lab to let us play on the computers. Miss Cotter's class is already in there, so Mr. Bergeron pairs us up. If Lynn were still my friend, she'd be my lab partner and would be whispering in my ear that Mr. Bergeron and Miss Cotter planned it this way so they could spend third period together. But Lynn is giggling with Nicole on the other side of the room.

"Monica, you're with Christine," Mr. Bergeron says.

Christine shrugs and we move our chairs as far apart as they can possibly be while still in front of the same computer.

"You can explore the Internet," he says. "But only the sites that fit the school's acceptable-policies code."

Miss Cotter points to Mr. Bergeron's tie, covered with waves and surfboards.

"You can surf the net." He holds his tie up for everyone to see. I smile at him, but no one else seems to notice his sad attempt at a joke except Miss Cotter, who thinks it's the funniest thing in the world. Maybe Lynn has a point after all.

Christine grabs the mouse. Our computer at home is old and doesn't have a modem, so the only time I get to search the Internet is at school. Judging by Christine's ease and fluid clicks of the mouse, she uses it all the time. I try not to be too obvious as I watch where she goes. Suddenly a crossword puzzle fills the monitor.

"*Boston Globe,*" she says. "You ever do it?"

"We don't get it," I answer.

"We don't either, but I check it on-line every day."

I study the screen, then watch her type in ARTERY.

"Five down is MANILA," I say.

We continue adding words until we can't do any more.

"Tough, huh?" Christine asks.

I nod, thinking that if Christine and I didn't hate each other, we'd probably have a lot in common. "We have time for a few more," she says.

Christine moves to another area of the net like a pro. Suddenly the words ANAGRAM GENERATOR fill the screen.

"What's that?" I ask.

"Haven't you used this before?" She seems surprised.

"No. What is it?"

"It makes anagrams. Isn't that how you always do them?"

"No. I do them in my head. I didn't think there was any other way," I answer.

"You do them in your *head*?" Half the class looks at us, so she lowers her voice. "How do you do them in your head?"

"I don't know. Practice, I guess. How does this work?"

She types in the word MONICA. I cringe, already knowing what the options are. And in a few seconds a list of anagrams appears.

"Nothing that good," she says. "IN COMA, that's pretty funny."

Not really.

"Let's put in your whole name." She types in the words MONICA DEVON. And—presto!—a list of words and phrases—over nine hundred of them!—fills the screen. I grab the mouse from Christine and scroll down. We read them together.

"DONOVAN MICE." Christine laughs. "NO MANIC DOVE."

I've made anagrams for my name lots of times before, but this is amazing. Most of the phrases are nonsense, of course, but every once in a while there's a great one. I have no idea how the computer is doing this; maybe some kind of math program. Letters, words flying across the screen— without attachment, without obsession. Just as they're meant to be.

"AVOID CON MEN!" I almost shout out loud. "ON ACID VENOM." When I come to another phrase, I stop and look at Christine. "MONICA DEVON—NO DAMN VOICE."

She shrugs. "How about you with CHRISTINE— NICE SHIRT?" she asks. "Like I didn't figure *that* out the first time you said it."

I feel my neck tense—*I've done something wrong, I'm get-*

ting caught, I'm going to get in trouble. But when I look at Christine, she's laughing. "I can't believe you didn't get NO DAMN VOICE till now. Gotcha."

I have to laugh too. Maybe the anagram is right after all. Maybe not having a strong voice of my own was part of the problem all along.

As I watch the words scroll down the screen—VANCE DOMINO, NOMADIC OVEN—I wish Grandpa were here. He'd *love* this. Maybe if I ask Mr. Bergeron, I can bring Grandpa with me to Parents' Night next year.

"You know what my favorite anagram is?" Christine asks. "MOTHER-IN-LAW—WOMAN HITLER."

"I just learned a new one from my grandpa. CLINT EASTWOOD—OLD WEST ACTION."

"That's a good one," Christine says. "Hey, wait." She enters PAUL BERGERON into the computer. I look over my shoulder to make sure he's not near us, then watch the words scroll.

"GO BURN A LEPER," I whisper. "PEEL A GRUB, RON."

Christine erupts in laughter. "RENE, BURP A LOG!"

Mr. Bergeron gives us both the "be quiet" face, then moves on. I'm in shock—I'm actually having fun with Christine. Being me.

Mr. Bergeron tells us to start heading back to class. "I can't believe you've been doing these in your head the whole time. Talk about doing things the hard way," Christine says.

"I like doing puzzles in my head," I say. "I'm going to be a cryptographer."

The conviction of this spontaneous response astounds me. Christine actually looks impressed. I type in my name again and look at the screen one more time. MONICA DEVON—not a group of letters jumbled up to make something else. It's me, it's all of me. Who I'll be forever.

Or at least for today.